MW00960057

Kidnapped

Kidnapped Idol

Jennie Bennett

To my husband, who made me a believer of true love.

Kidnapped Idol

A K-pop Romance Book

This book is a work of fiction. Names, characters, places and incidents are either the product of the author's imagination or used fictitiously. Any resemblance to actual persons living or dead, or to actual events or locales is entirely coincidental.

ISBN-10: 1543150225

ISBN-13: 978-1543150223

Editing by Precy Larkins

Printed in the United States of America

CONTENTS

Being Prepared

~~1. Visit the Great Wall of China~~

"Jenica, are you really crossing that off your list, right this second?" Blain says, scrunching her nose and causing her stud to glint in the sun.

I put the cap back on my pen and shove it into my shoulder bag. "Yeah, why not?"

Blain gives me her classic nasty-face, which always makes me giggle. "Because we just showed up. You haven't really done it yet."

"Being here is doing it," I argue. "Even if it's just the parking lot."

If it wasn't so crowded I'd take a second to enjoy that I'm really here, at the Great Wall of China like I always dreamed. As it is, I'm being jostled between the masses, pushed so roughly I can't even see ten feet in front of me. The smell of exhaust from all the buses and cars is overwhelming. Stupid tourist season.

Blain shakes her head, her short bubble-gum pink hair staying in its gelled perfection. She's not afraid to stand out. If her hair wasn't enough, the purple lipstick and ripped leggings would give it away.

I, on the other hand, am wearing my usual buttoned-to-the-chin white shirt and jeans. Okay, I'm wearing a cardigan too. It's navy blue because Blain keeps begging me to try more colors.

Before I put my notebook away, I look over my list one last time. It's always good to double check.

1. ~~Visit the Great Wall of China~~
2. Do something that makes me uncomfortable
3. Eat a crazy food from a street vendor
4. Skip class
5. Fall in love

Okay, so maybe I've made some hefty goals for myself. I didn't intend to write the last one, but I decided I was going to be honest and put down the thing I really wanted to do. I was listening to my favorite song, Ed Sheeran's *Kiss Me* as I wrote it and I got sentimental. I don't expect to cross everything off while I'm in China, but it would be nice.

Blain tugs me out of the way before I can be trampled by more tourists disembarking. "Your list can wait until we get back to the dorm."

I brush away a stray black hair that's blown in my face. "No," I counter. "I can't. It's part of the rules–once an item has been accomplished it must be checked off."

Blain shakes her head, smirk on her lips. "You are such a nerd."

She's one to talk. She was the only white girl back in Oklahoma to ace Mandarin. Since my heritage is Chinese, I was raised speaking it at home. Mandarin was supposed to be an easy A for me, and it was, but Blain still got a higher final score.

If she wasn't my best friend, I might be upset she took the valedictorian spot with that grade. But it's okay, I still got salutatorian.

"Suck it up," I say to Blain, tapping her super-tiny waist with my notebook. "You know you wanted to come here, too. Even if it's touristy."

"I guess," Blain says, obviously trying to play it cool.

She used to intimidate the crap out of me before I got to know her, but now I see her as nothing more than a bear stuffed with fluff.

Blain shrugs. "The live music over there isn't so bad."

I hadn't noticed the stage until Blain pointed it out. She's five-foot-eight and I'm four inches shorter than that. I assumed the pop music was coming from speakers somewhere.

To be honest, the Great Wall of China isn't what I was expecting. Sure, I knew it would be busy; China is the most populated country on the planet. What I didn't expect was all the vendors. Everywhere I look, someone is trying to sell me something. Cotton candy, stuffed animals, even Great Wall of China balloons. Feels ninety percent amusement park and ten percent historical monument.

I stuff my notebook back in my bag and pull out my handy guidebook *China: A Walk Through Asia's Heartland* flipping to the tab of the Great Wall.

"It says here," I read to Blain, "if we hike far enough, the people will thin out. I bet there's some incredible views."

Blain snatches the volume from me, slapping it closed as she goes. "Jenica. Let's put the books away and enjoy ourselves."

I want to. Really. But I also feel the overwhelming urge to be prepared for anything. My stomach has been doing the butterfly dance since we first boarded the bus in Beijing. I have no idea why I'm so nervous, but I can't seem to settle myself.

"Fine," I say, taking a deep breath. Because I know Blain is right. She usually is. "I'll keep my bag closed for the rest of the day. Promise."

"Thank you," Blain says with a hint of a smile. "Now come on, let's get hiking."

Sure enough, it only takes us twenty minutes of walking to leave the crowds. The amusement park aura hasn't left, however. Thankfully, we're able to worm past the zoo section—for real, there were even Monkeys—but we're still passing little stands with old men selling granola bars and water.

After thirty minutes, I end up breaking my promise to Blain by opening my bag. It's not to get a book, though. The views are so breathtaking I have to photograph my surroundings.

My camera was the one thing I insisted on bringing with me. The study abroad counselor told us to pack sparingly, but I couldn't leave my camera even if it's the size of a small dog.

I stop in the middle of a dip between two towers, getting caught up in the lush green hills. Clouds move in at a steady pace, making for incredible picture taking. Overcast skies create great lighting, too.

I swing the lens around to Blain who immediately throws her hands over her face. She doesn't seem to understand she's one of the prettiest girls I've ever met. She could be on the cover of a magazine and no one would question it.

"Come on, Blain, just a couple snaps?" I beg.

Her hands don't budge. "No, you're always taking horrid pictures of me."

"Hardly," I say. "Your pictures always come out flawless."

"Whatever," Blain says into her palms.

I point the camera down so she doesn't feel threatened. "How about we make a deal?" I ask, batting my eyelashes. Blain hates it when I do that.

She peeks between her fingers. "What kind of deal?"

"You let me snap one picture, and you can pick what we do tomorrow."

Her arms go slack. "Really? But I'm picking what we do tonight."

I take in a deep breath. "I'll do both. I can let go sometimes, too."

Blain spreads her arms. “Snap away.”

I take a few in fast succession as Blain poses.

“All right,” Blain says, pointing at me. “That’s enough.”

I snap a few more of her finger pointed towards my camera.

“Jenica Marie Lee,” she says. “You better quit it.”

“You’ll have to catch me first,” I tease, backing up. I keep snapping as she charges at me.

She’s not really trying because she knows how much this camera means to me. Her angry faces will make awesome pictures.

Since she knows she can’t win, she decides to take the flight approach. I’m capturing her running to the next tower—uphill, no less—when I’m startled by a drop of water on my head.

I turn my face to the sky as two more drops hit my cheeks. There’s no way I’m letting my camera get wet if it’s raining. I stuff it in my bag to keep it dry before glancing at Blain. She’s already made it to the top of the hill, and she's shaking her head at me like she knows I won't be able to make it to her before it starts pouring.

"Later!" I scream so she knows I'll catch up when it dries out.

There was no rain in the forecast. I know because I checked a million times this morning. Stupid weather-people.

The rain, which started slow, picks up until it's falling in freezing sheets. I sprint uphill in the opposite direction of Blain, but it's not as steep on this side.

I'm hunched over in an attempt to protect my camera as I lunge for the tower entrance. This ends up being a crap move as the stone is slick when wet.

My arms fly forward as my sneakers lose their grip. I try to regain my balance, but in the process I end up twisting my left ankle. My right knee takes the impact first, with my left elbow hitting before I can catch myself.

I stay flat on my stomach for a second to catch my breath. Using my non-existent army-crawl skills, I pull myself the rest of the way into the tower. I want to stand, but as soon as I put pressure on my left ankle, I yelp in pain.

Grabbing the wall for support, I slide to a sitting position in the narrow walkway. Only one person can hike through at a time. Even then, the walls seem to close in.

Blain is like me when it comes to rain. My mom always told me I'd get sick if so much as a drop touched my head, and so as a child I was afraid of it. Now it's not as terrible, but I still don't like it.

Blain has different reasons, but I'm sure she's hunkering down all the same. Hopefully it'll leave as quickly as it started. We have a half-hour walk back, and my ankle is throbbing.

Lightning flashes, and I let out an involuntary scream. A shadow stands in the opening opposite me, backlit by the sudden burst of light.

I scream again when the thunder booms, this time attempting to stand as the shadowy figure enters the space. This is not how I'm supposed to die. I only got to check the first item off my list. I have so much ahead of me.

"It's okay," the probably-murderer says to me in Chinese. "I'm only getting out of the rain."

Lightning strikes again, and this time I see a hint of the guy's face. He doesn't look like a gangster, but I still don't trust him.

I put my weight on my good foot and hop backwards. "You just stay over there. If you so much as touch me, I'll call the police."

My hand reaches in my bag for my phone to make my point. I hold it up to show him, and then get the idea to take a picture just in case the police need evidence.

The flash goes off as I hit the button, and the dude stumbles at the bright light.

"What the crap was that for?" he shouts.

"Stay away or investigators will be able to track you down through my phone."

I'm expecting more anger, but instead, he laughs. "Okay," he says, holding up his hands. "I promise to keep to my side."

I feel a little better, but I still hold my phone out like a weapon, just in case. The space isn't that big. If he wanted to get at me it wouldn't take much.

"You know," he says, "if you have a flashlight on that phone, we could make a lamp."

"What do you mean?" I ask, not moving even though my good leg is starting to get sore.

"I saw it on a show once," he says. "If you put your flashlight under a water bottle, it can light up a whole room."

That doesn't sound so dangerous. I keep my eyes on him as I riffle through my bag for my bottle. It's only about half full, but hopefully it'll still work.

The flashlight is pretty bright on its own, but the second I put it under my water bottle something incredible happens. I might as well have flipped on a light switch for how bright it is. But that's not the cool part. Because my water bottle is blue, it looks like we're totally submerged in the clearest lake. With the sound of the rain outside I might as well be. It's calming.

"This is amazing," I say, turning my attention from the walls to my tower-buddy.

For the first time I can see him clearly. He's not murderer material at all. In fact, he's more like puppy material. He has adorable smiling eyes and full lips that turn up in the corners. His thick hair is all messed up from the rain, but the cut is really nice so it looks more casual-cool than bed head.

My face heats up for no reason whatsoever. I guess if lightning can make a person look ominous, streaks of water-light can make a person look beautiful.

It isn't until he moves his gaze from my eyes to the floor that I realize I'm staring. Super bad idea. I'm not sure where all my common sense went. He's still a complete stranger.

If anyone could win an award for being weird around strangers, it would be me.

Taking Risks

▶▷▶

I lean against the wall, hoping to support myself. The sound of rain highlights how quiet it is, but I have nothing to say. "Rain, eh?" isn't exactly a stunning conversation starter.

"I–"

"You–"

We say at the same time.

I stay quiet so he can talk, but he stays quiet too, leaving nothing but weight between us.

My good leg aches so I try to shift positions, but I end up putting weight on my sprain. I wince as I draw in a breath through my teeth.

The guy reaches out a hand, but seems to remember to keep his distance.

"Are you okay?" he asks, keeping firmly to his space.

"Yeah," I say, even though it's not true. "I just slipped a little in the rain." Since I'm pretty sure this guy's not going to kill me, I decide to sit again.

"You..." he starts, pausing as if to gather his words. "You don't know who I am, do you?"

I look in his eyes and feel myself getting warm again. "No," I say. Because I don't.

He sighs, and it looks like he's relaxing for the first time since he came into my tower. "That's good," he answers with a nod.

I nod with him, even though I don't know what I'm nodding about.

He sits cross-legged, facing me. I can tell he wants to ask me something more, so I stay quiet.

"You really don't recognize my face?" he asks again. "Even a little?"

This is getting weird now. "No. I don't. But I'm not Chinese." I don't know why I felt the need to add that part, but it seems relevant.

"I mean," I correct. "I am Chinese. But I'm from America. I've only been here for three days now." Why am I still talking? *Shut your mouth, Jenica.*

He smiles, his eyes turning to half-moons. "That makes sense, then." He says this in English, and his English is way better than his Mandarin.

"I grew up in Hong Kong mostly speaking English, but I took Mandarin classes while living there, too," he explains when he sees my face.

I smile back, feeling like a total idiot. I shouldn't have made the assumption.

"In that case," the guy continues, extending a hand. "I'm Woon."

Woon? Doesn't sound like a Chinese name. I wonder if he has another ethnicity in him. Korean, maybe?

"Jenica," I respond, hesitantly taking his hand and shaking. It's warm, and my fingers are freezing.

He points to my foot. "Do you mind if I take a look at your ankle?"

I'm a little weirded out, but I'm also worried I won't make it back to the buses in this condition. "Um," I say, not ready to give in. "Are you a doctor?"

"Hardly," Woon says. "But there's a lot of ankle injuries in my profession."

What kind of profession? "So you're an athlete?" I guess.

He looks at the light playing across the ceiling as he contemplates. "Sort of."

I stare at the ceiling too. We're alone, and he hasn't done anything but be kind. Not only is my ankle hurting, but my knee and elbow have taken a beating, too. I still have to get home at some point. If I'm going to do that, I need his help.

"Go ahead," I say like I don't care, even though I do.

He shuffles closer to me, hands hovering over my injury. "Let me know if it hurts."

I suck in a breath, readying myself for the pain.

"Don't worry," he says. "I'll be gentle."

There's talking, and there's doing. I'll reserve my judgement until he proves it.

His touch is so soft my shoulders ease away from my ears, body relaxing. He nudges at my sock, pulling it down to expose the skin.

"Still okay?" he asks when my ankle is totally bare.

It's just my foot, but I feel a tad naked. "Yeah." My voice comes out all wobbly.

His fingers prod at the flesh near the bone. "No discomfort?"

"It's a little sore, but not unbearable," I answer, barely managing to keep my tone level.

"Now," he says, raising his head so we make eye contact. "I'm going to move your foot. Let me know if it hurts. I don't want to push it."

Is this a bad time for me to notice he's beautiful? Because he is. Truly.

He eases my toes toward me, and I cringe but don't cry out. He takes his time moving my foot forward and back, side to side. I can handle the ache, even if it still hurts.

"Good news," he says. "Nothing is broken, but you'll still want to rest your foot today."

I nod, but can't seem to find the right words. I'm so awkward around guys. My only boyfriend didn't ask me out for months because he thought I hated him. It wasn't until I started opening up that he finally had the courage to tell me how he felt. Neither of us knew how to communicate, which left the relationship doomed.

Basically, I'm going to be single forever.

"That rain was really someth–" Blain interjects as she walks in.

I've been so lost in Woon's eyes, I didn't notice the rain stopping.

"Hello," Blain says to Woon, narrowing her gaze at him.

Crap. She's about to get territorial. I have to jump in before she yells at him for touching me. Because ankles are so sexy.

"Blain," I say, giving her my stop-before-you-embarrass-me voice. "This is Woon. I hurt myself running in here, and he was helping."

Blain doesn't uncross her arms or lower her chin. This is going to take real damage control.

Woon slowly lets go of my foot and backs to his side of the tower. He gives Blain a quick bow, saying hello in Chinese and English.

"I should go," he says. "It was nice to meet you, Jenica."

Already? But I was just about to get over my shyness. "Likewise," I respond, bumbling the word.

He points behind Blain, who's still standing in the entryway. "I'm going that way."

After all the rain, he's still hiking on? Why?

Blain moves to let him by, keeping silent. Her expression has softened a bit, but she won't stop staring at Woon.

"Could you help me up?" I ask Blain, not wanting to put too much weight on my foot.

"Yeah," she says, still watching Woon.

After I gather my stuff, she puts my arm around her neck. We stand together, and I lean on her as we hobble out of the tower.

Blain's so much taller than me I know she must be hurting, but she doesn't complain. I don't complain either, even though it's awkward and every bit of weight shoots pain up my leg. At our current pace it'll take us three times as long to get back. I hope it doesn't rain again.

"We can rest," I say when we get to the next tower.

Both of us are panting. This isn't going to work. I'll have to try and walk on my own through the pain. It might make it worse, but we're low on options.

Blain pulls out her water bottle and sips while we catch our breath. I take a drink, too, hoping what I have left will survive the rest of the hike.

"That guy," Blain says after a moment of silence. "He looks familiar."

"Does he?" I ask, remembering the way she watched him leave.

"Yeah." Blain tucks her water bottle in her backpack. "I know I've seen him somewhere before."

Huh. That's weird because I swear I would recognize him if I saw him again.

Blain turns her head to glace at the way we came. "Speak of the devil and the devil shall appear."

I furrow my brow. "What?"

"That dude who helped you is running back here."

My cheeks warm. "You better not be messing with me, Blain. He just left."

Blain shakes her head. "I wish I was. Take a look for yourself."

I lean around her, and sure enough, Woon is headed full speed in our direction. Weird.

"Excuse me," I say, pushing past Blain to the outside.

Woon slows his pace when he sees me. He also smiles. Why does that make my stomach spin?

"Woon?" My voice is a pitch too high, and I know it.

He stops right outside my personal bubble. A little too far away.

"You shouldn't be putting weight on that," he says, pointing to my ankle.

I laugh. Where did he come from?

"I know," I say, because I'm smooth like that.

If I were to speak my mind, I'd ask him why he came back to me. Luckily, my filter is working well enough for me to know I'm not the center of the universe. Maybe he just went the wrong direction and he was running because he had to double back.

"I mean," I correct, trying to get my bearings. "Blain has been helping me, but it's slow going."

"That's okay," he says. "If you'd gone faster, I'm not sure I'd have been able to catch up to you."

So he *was* coming back for me. I hope the red in my cheeks isn't showing, even though my face is on fire.

"Well," I respond with my usual flare. "You found me."

He smiles, looking at the ground, and then back up at me. "Yes, I did."

I'm pretty sure heart rates drop when resting, so I don't know why mine is suddenly kicking into overdrive.

"I was thinking," he continues, rubbing the back of his neck. "You could help me."

My teeth snap together to hold in my immediate reply of, "Anything!" Instead, I let my sensible side rule by taking a second to think. I place my hand on the side of the tower entrance so I can put less weight on my foot. "What do you need help with?"

He meets my gaze, clear brown eyes bright. "It might take me all day to get where I'm going. Which is fine, but it could be faster if I call someone. That's when I remembered you have a phone. Do you mind?"

My chest tightens as my heartbeat slows. My phone. Of course. All he needed me for was my phone. He had no other reason to return, and I was stupid enough to entertain the fantasy for one brief second. This is why I never let impulsive Jenica out of her room.

"Of course," I say, shaking my head as I reach into my bag.

I hope my outside doesn't look how my inside feels, because my inside feels like it's weeping.

My phone is conservative like me. It's a smartphone, but an older model. I have a simple black case and an unassuming background. Unlike Blain's, which is glittery and loud.

I swipe it open, and halfway through punching in my code the phone goes dark. I forgot how quickly the flashlight drains the battery.

"Crap," I say, trying to punch it back to life. "Blain, let me see your phone."

My hand is behind me waiting for her to put it in my palm. When nothing happens, my gaze travels to her face. She's pouting.

"What?" I ask, afraid of the answer.

Blain pulls her arms to her chest and turns sideways like she's scared I'm going to hit her. "I left my phone at the dorm."

So typical of Blain. I don't even know why her parents bought her such an expensive one. She always forgets it.

"I'm sorry," I say to Woon.

He won't look at me, and it's making me feel small. I should be used to it since I'm only five-four, but it stings.

"It's okay," he says, but his actions say otherwise.

I can't believe I'm about to tell him this, but I hate that he's hurt. "If you really need a phone, you can come back with us and we'll get you one."

"No," he says while shaking his head. "It's too risky."

Risky? The way he says that word makes me think he's in trouble. Maybe it's better if we part ways. I'd rather not rock the boat.

I point behind me even though he's not looking in my direction. "Blain and I really need to get back, so..."

"Yeah," he says, nodding his head. "Don't let me keep you."

That's it then. There's nothing more to say.

I try to turn around, but it proves difficult with one foot. Habit kicks in and I put my injured ankle into normal walking position. I'm not ready for the pain, and I end up over-correcting my balance, which throws me backward rather than keeping me upright.

I'm going to fall and I have no idea how to stop it. My arms circle the air like I'm trying to fly, but I'm obviously not built for aerodynamics. I can just picture my face turning into a #fail gif meme.

Before my head can hit the bricks, arms surround my waist, my back pressing into muscle behind me. I turn my head to see Woon's face right next to mine, a hint of dimple on his cheek.

I can feel everything. The definition in his chest, the grip of his arms around me, his breath on my skin. He smells like rice, honey, and spices. It reminds me of home.

There's always a moment when eye contact goes from nice to awkward, and the second I hit that limit I look away. Rationality dictates that Woon should let go of me. He needs to get to wherever, and I have to go back to the dorms on a bad foot.

The only things I know about him is that he can make a lamp from simple things, and he's in shape. Must come with his athletic career, whatever that may be.

Rationality, however, seems to be something Woon isn't aware of. He slides his hands across my stomach, and I suck in as goosebumps tickle from the point of contact up my body. His fingers grip my hips as he slips his head under my arm. Hope I don't stink.

"You need to stop trying to walk on that foot," he says, laughter in his eyes.

The only thing going on in my head is brain static. I've been completely paralyzed by Woon. I pride myself on my smarts, but right now I don't know how to speak. For once, I'm glad my day isn't going according to plan.

Tainted Memories

▶▷▶

"I really shouldn't," he whispers to me. "But I'll help you get back to the buses."

"Okay," I squeak out, the fuzz in my thoughts keeping me from saying anything more.

"Blain," Woon calls. "Why don't you get on her other side so we can get you back faster."

Yes. Good idea. That way I won't have to lean so heavily on Woon. Then maybe I'll be able to get a sentence together.

"Wait," Woon says as Blain starts to approach. "Do either of you have a hat or scarf or something? It would be better if I could hide my face."

Who has a scarf in August? It's sweltering enough out here, especially with the humidity from the recent rain.

"Sorry–" I start, but Blain cuts me off.

"I have a baseball cap, but it's purple."

"That'll work," Woon says. "Do you have sunglasses too?"

"Only if you like rhinestones," Blain replies.

Woon raises his eyebrows. "I'm not averse to them."

Who is this guy?

Blain puts her accessories on him, and I can't hold back my snickering. He looks adorable in that get-up.

"Shall we?" I say as Blain supports my other side.

This is so much easier with Woon helping. He's pretty much carrying me through most of this hike, and he's not even breaking a sweat. I would think he's a weightlifter, but his muscles aren't bulging like guys who spend too much time at the gym. He's not a skinny noodle either. There's no apt description for him other than perfect. Which puts him miles out of my league.

"Let's rest for a bit," Woon says when we can see the crowd from a distance.

"I'm gonna sit." Blain points inside the nearest tower.

I nod, supporting myself on the wall. Since she's doing most of the work I should let her have the stairs.

Woon comes next to me, leaning over to look at the landscape on the other side.

I share my water with him because he doesn't have anything. Who hikes that far out without a pack? Especially if he was planning on hiking all day.

Even with his eyes covered by the sunglasses, I can see the worry in his brow as he looks towards the exit.

"What are you running from?" I ask. It's just a guess, but it makes the most sense.

He gulps the last of my water down, still not looking at me properly. I wait as he breathes. Locks of his silky hair get picked up by the wind.

"Bad guys," he says in all seriousness.

I laugh, but he doesn't join me.

"What kind of bad guys?" I prod, resting the side of my face on my fist.

His eyes flit to mine then back to the view. "The kind nice girls shouldn't get involved in."

My spine straightens as I twist around to put my back to the wall. Of course he already has me pegged as a teacher's pet. He's not wrong, but all the excitement had me hoping he'd see me differently.

I know I'm the stereotype for an Asian girl with no looks. If I don't have my nose in a book, I'm probably still thinking about facts. I'm never the party girl. And I'm certainly not the type to get caught up with a bad boy. Sometimes I wish people could see me for who I am. I'm not sure what that is, but it's more than a bookworm.

"Honestly," he says, still studying the view. "If I can make it on a bus back to Beijing, my life might be saved."

That sounds ominous. Is he for real?

"Enough about me," he continues, straightening up. "We should get you back."

This time, when he puts his arm around me, the mood has shifted. I'm not very good at comforting people, but I give him a gentle friend-zone squeeze. "It's going to be okay. We'll get you back."

He smiles, but there's no feeling behind it. "I hope so."

We hobble over to Blain who takes my other side. She keeps shooting me glances and tipping her head at Woon while raising her eyebrows. In best friend, speak it means are-you-into-him?

I open my eyes wide in response, clenching my jaw. That means, you're-embarrassing-me-stop.

Woon gets jittery as we enter the crowd. His head is hung low and he's walking closer to me than he was before. I shift position to help cover his face. If he really is in trouble, I should do what I can. Unless he's a criminal.

Oh gosh. What if he expected me to recognize him because he's been on the evening news or something? Or maybe there are wanted posters hung around Beijing. What if my first instinct was right and I'm aiding and abetting a murderer? He did say bad people were after him.

Then again, I don't see hardened criminal anywhere in that sweet face of his. It's not like he's asking me to hide him. If we get on the bus and head back to the city, we can separate then. If he's wanted by the police, I doubt he can hide there.

His grip on my waist tightens as he passes the outdoor stage. Whatever band was there is packing up, twenty burly security guards standing around them with nothing to do but look intimidating.

"It's going to be okay," I say to him. "We're almost there."

"Yeah," he responds, but his hold doesn't loosen.

We wait in a line of people to board, Woon not looking up once. When we're at the front, Woon lets go of me to get in the bus first, and then helps me after him.

The next thing happens so fast, it's a blur. All it takes is one look—the second his head pops up to see the bus driver, I can tell it's over.

"Maximus!" she shouts. "Is it really you?"

Woon makes shushing motions, but it's too late. A few heads have turned and then people are rushing us.

Screams fill the air, with girls crying for Maximus who I guess is Woon. He tries to push past the crowd to get on the bus, but they push back. I'm suffocating in a sea of bodies. I would fall down, but there's no room to move.

If Blain didn't have a firm hold of me, I'd be afraid to lose her.

Just as quickly as the crowd descends on us, they flee at the sound of whistles. Woon takes the opportunity to jump on the bus, but the security guards from the music place grab him and drag him off. Blain's sunglasses fall in the dirt, and I catch Woon's gaze one last time before he's being shoved into a bus with CSTAR written across the side.

"What the crap was that about?" Blain says.

I shake my head, my nerves still on edge. "I have no idea."

Blain slaps a magazine in front of me. "I knew it."

The semester starts in two days and I'm busy reading all of the syllabi so I can schedule my study time. We didn't get to do what Blain wanted because of my foot, which has healed enough for me to walk slowly.

"Knew what?" I say, not glancing up from highlighting.

"That guy the other day," she says, sitting on my creaky-spring bed.

My face goes hot as I think of Woon, but I try to swallow my emotions. I wish I could've done something more to help, but a petite girl like me has nothing on burly dudes in suits.

"Woon?" I say, pretending I don't care, even though I'm itching to see that magazine.

"Maximus," Blain corrects. "I knew I'd seen him before. He's on the cover of Beijing's biggest gossip rag."

I toss the syllabus I was staring at and pick up the thick glossy volume. There's no point in concentrating anymore.

"This is Woon?" I say, pointing to the guy on the cover.

His shirt is half open, eyes lined black, and hair styled up out of his face. He looks like he belongs on that cover. Nothing like the guy I met.

"Read it!" Blain says.

I'm not perfect at reading Mandarin, but Blain is worse when she's nervous. She can study well, but in real life it's harder. MAXIMUS is written in bold across the bottom of the page in English with the phrase "hottest new China star." Below it, in Chinese characters.

I flip to the contents, trying to get there quickly.

"Well?" Blain says, her fidgeting legs racking at my nerves.

Holy.

I tip the volume so Blain can see. There's a half-page picture of Woon lying on his side, elbow to the ground and head propped in his hand. He's wearing a navy blue knit suit, and it looks amazing on him. His tie is *just* undone with the top bottom unhooked. I think I'm drooling.

"Wow," Blain says. "He looks hot."

As if I needed her to tell me.

I scan the article and start reading when it gets to the meat of the story. "In a bold move, Maximus has left his Korean agency and *Speeders*—one of the top groups in all of South East Asia. Rumor has it, he's joined forces with CSTAR for a solo debut and a leap up in his acting career."

I raise my eyes to see Blain's reaction, but she's on her phone. How can she not freak out about this? As far as I saw it, CSTAR kidnapped him. If this article is true, why was he running?

"What are you doing?" I say to Blain, trying not to explode.

Blain scrolls furiously. "I'm searching him. What else do you think I'm doing?"

My shoulders slump. "Oh."

I continue to scan the article, flipping the slick paper as I go. There's a full-page spread of Woon with some girl putting her hands all over him. The girl's face is either in shadow or cut off completely, but it's obvious she's beautiful. I hate the way she's touching him. Especially with his soul-gazing expression. It makes no sense to be jealous over a guy I've only met once.

"I'll tell you this," Blain says, still looking at her phone. "People in Korea are not happy."

I wish I could see Woon and ask him what's going on, but the probability of finding him is pretty much zilch.

Music starts, and Blain motions me to sit next to her. YouTube is open, and I read the title of the song just under the video. Most of it is in Korean, but *Speeders* is very clearly written in English. The song is catchy. I don't know what I was expecting, but it wasn't this.

Of course I've heard of Kpop. I'm young and Asian, it's impossible to avoid. But I've done everything I can not to get sucked into it. I have enough distractions from my studies.

Within the first minute, I can tell I'm a goner. I've seen bits and pieces of other music videos, but I've never sat down and watched one all the way through. I count seven boys, all dancing in perfect sync. The song rocks, too.

When the camera zooms in on Woon, I hold my breath. I thought he was good looking before, but all dressed up he's on a totally different level.

I stand, knocking Blain's phone as I go. "I don't want to watch anymore," I say, panic rising in my throat. The dorm is already small, and now it feels like a box. "I'm going to get some air."

How did I get caught up in this? The last thing I want is to worry about a guy I don't even know.

Short of finding CSTAR headquarters and marching in there, there's no way to find Woon, anyhow. Whatever's going on with him shouldn't matter to me. I'm here to study Mandarin and live in a foreign country for a year. Nothing more.

I take the elevator down and slam open the gate to the outside. Because the school is next to a major thoroughfare, there's nowhere to go here for peace and quiet. People are everywhere and the city constantly buzzes with life. It's not like I can breathe fresh air either, not with all the smog. Some people wear masks over their faces on a daily basis.

I knew all this going in, but right now I really miss the open Oklahoma skies. Eighteen years of my life were spent in a little country town filled with farms. I had one year at Oklahoma State, which is a pinprick compared to this city.

At least at OSU, I could go home to my family on the weekends. Adult or not, I wish I had my mom here. I can call her, but that would mean going back upstairs to get my phone.

I decide to walk instead. Even if it's all hustle and bustle, at least I'll fit into the streams of people.

What would my mom say if she was here? She didn't really want me leaving, but she couldn't stop me so she supported me. She would probably tell me to not worry about boys and focus on what really mattered, and she would be right.

The streets are huge, but not big enough to escape like I want. It's beautiful in its own way, but nothing like what I'm used to.

I pass a coffee shop–I swear there's one on every corner–and decide to stop for a smoothie. I don't have cash with me but luckily I've gotten into the habit of wearing my debit card on a necklace wallet all the time, but only because my mom told me to.

"One Raspberry Blast," I say to the cashier. It's almost five U.S. dollars, but so worth it when it comes to thinking juice.

The coffee shops aren't that different from back home, thankfully. I can feel a bit of America with me when I come here.

I take a seat by the window to wait. Outside, faces pass me by, drawn in their own thoughts, struggling with their own problems. Half of them are staring at their phones.

This is how we live. The world is what it is. We have friends and family, but ultimately, we're on our own. Woon is a huge pop star. Whatever's going on with him doesn't require me.

"Raspberry Blast," the cashier calls, and I rush to the front to get my drink.

I take a sip, and my eyes are drawn to the television behind the counter. It's hard to ignore the bright colors and flashing screen. Once again, I find myself faced with Woon in *Speeder*. It's not the same video as before, but just as impressionable as the other.

How do they dance so perfectly?

"Speeder fan?" Someone says behind me in a mix between Mandarin and English. Mandrish?

It's a teen girl, still dressed in her school uniform. I shake my head, but say nothing more. She points at the screen during a close-up. "That's my bias, V6."

I smile at her, even though I have no idea what a bias is.

"Everyone likes Maximus," she continues without prompting. "Just because he's half Chinese. But V6 is the most handsome."

"I think I've seen Maximus before," I say. I don't know why I'm entertaining this conversation when I should just leave, but I'm curious all the same.

"You have," she responds matter-of-factly.

She points out the window behind me, and sure enough, there's a huge picture of Woon advertising a swanky watch. Weird. I have the sudden urge to buy one.

"It's such a joke about him leaving Speeder," the girl continues. "He would never."

I furrow my brow. "Why is that?"

"Look at him," she says. "He loves his group."

She nods her head at the screen, and it's a scene of all the boys rough-housing at the beach. They look close.

The girl sighs. "I don't get it. He would never leave his best friends."

Cashier lady hands the teen her drink. With a swoop of long black hair, I'm alone again.

Even when the music video ends I still see it playing in my head. Close-ups of Woon looking amazing. Unreal. God like. He's someone I can't begin to understand or touch. My conversation with the girl has cemented how very little I know about him. So why can't I get him out of my head.

I slurp the last of my drink and crush my cup. This is the last straw. I'll just have to try and forget all the things I've felt for him. If only I can get my heart to comply.

Getting Out

"Please," Blain begs. "We've been stuck in this dorm for a week straight."

It's true, but I still don't have time to go out. The work load is heavier than I anticipated, and I have some catching up to do even though the semester's just begun.

I think of number four on my list, but push it aside. I will skip class, but not anytime soon. Not until I can get it all under control.

"Maybe tomorrow," I say, turning back to my books.

"Jenica," she chides, slamming her hand over the section I'm reading. "I'm all for studying, but we have to get out sometimes, too."

I try to shove her hand away, but she keeps it firm.

"Just let me finish this," I beg.

Blain pushes my swivel chair around to face her. "You know why I was valedictorian?

Because I knew when I needed a break. Jenica, you can't keep burning yourself out."

I do get really intense when it comes to studying, but I'm also afraid of leaving. Every time I go outside I see Woon everywhere. He's in a billion ads and his music videos are played in almost every shop I walk into. I even recognize some of the songs now and sing along with the English chorus. My plan to forget him has totally backfired.

Woon has some serious pipes. Not that I've been paying attention to that. He's too famous for me. I shouldn't have to remind myself daily.

Blain sighs. "I know we're here for the next eight months, but what if our chances of getting out grow smaller as the school year goes on? Please."

She's right. I shouldn't keep her from having a good time because I'm afraid of seeing Woon somewhere.

"Okay," I say, realizing if I'm going to skip a class, now is the time. I pull out my notebook and start to cross off number four—skip a class. "But can I pick the place?" If we're lucky I can finish off number three as well—eat a crazy food from a street vendor.

Blain grabs my hands and bounces, her blue eyes sparkling. "Thank you, thank you, thank you."

"Whatever," I say. "Let me grab my jacket."

It's not terribly cold, but it's been raining on and off a lot so I've been taking a raincoat everywhere I go. I don't want a repeat of what happened on the Great Wall. This coat is big enough to pull over my camera which I've hung around my neck. I laugh as I glance down. Black jacket, black polo, black camera, at least my jeans are blue. I slip on my comfiest sneakers and pull my long dark hair into a ponytail. Not hip, but me.

The street market is in the middle of Beijing, about an hour away by metro. There's not much to see on the train as it's underground, but I don't mind the trip because there's plenty of people to watch. Never in my life did I picture myself here. Sure, I was the one who made this happen, but it still feels dream like.

When we arrive, I start to bounce with excitement. This is probably the thing I've been looking forward to most.

I gasp as we emerge from the underground and take in the view. Lights from the palace glimmer in the distance, the Tongzi River reflecting the city. It's like stepping into a Chinese fairytale, only with more people.

It's a short walk from the stop to the market, and I can already tell it's a busy Friday night. Crowded as the city is, it's not usually this insane. I don't mind, though, it's great to see so many people out.

This isn't like the rest of the city so far. The crowd here is a lot more diverse. There are at least five different languages spoken as we near the market, and many more when we get there.

"Should we try some bug on a stick?" Blain says, in all seriousness.

I snap a picture of the rows of skewers—everything from beetle to spider—before I look up.

"Yes!" I answer, putting the camera down and pulling out my notebook. "As long as we follow it with something edible."

Blain gets in line ahead of me—she's always willing to be adventurous. I pick something that doesn't look too bad but still fits my crazy criteria: starfish.

It tastes like the sea, really salty and a little fishy. Since it's been deep fried, it has that familiar American grease too. It's not the worst thing I've ever put in my mouth.

As we walk, we spot everything from fresh veggies to silkworms, but Blain doesn't stop until we see some steamed buns.

I order pork and Blain gets red bean. We take our time strolling as we eat. This how I imagined city life. Neon lights, hanging lanterns, and a crowd of locals and tourists alike.

Add to that the perfect weather, and the place is packed.

Blain and I try some fruit-on-a-stick that's covered in a hard sugar glaze. It's pretty amazing, even with the overwhelming ocean smell dominating the marketplace.

Without meaning to, Blain and I drift to the sound of pumping bass. If I thought the throng was bad before, it was nothing like the mob standing around the stage. Flooded by hot stage lights are three girls wearing tiny skirts and dancing cutesy.

I'm about to drag Blain away when I spot the logo on the backdrop of the stage. CSTAR in all its glory. It even has a giant shooting star under the letters, as if it wasn't cheesy enough.

"Isn't that–?" Blain says, and I nod before she can finish.

There's no reason for me to wish Woon here. He doesn't even like girls. But...I can't seem to escape him. It's been a week, and I notice him in everything. It doesn't help that his face is plastered everywhere, but it's more than that.

As hard as I work to bury my mind in school, I find myself daydreaming about that day on the Great Wall. Okay, so maybe in my dreams we do a little more than put our arms around each other, but that's why it's not reality.

But if he *is* here...

"What's going through your head, Jenica?" Blain asks, her words hard.

She's never this brisk with me and it snaps me out of my thoughts. "I'm sorry," I say, even though I haven't done anything.

Blain shakes her head, eyes wide. "Woon is a celebrity."

She doesn't have to point that out. "I know."

Blain gestures at the stage. "You can't get involved in his life. From what I read online, he chose CSTAR. You have to let him live with that choice."

"I know!" I snap back, because I do.

She's not the only one who's searched his name since that day. I've read everything about how his Chinese heritage separated him from the other members, and all the conjecture about him abandoning *Speeders* because of fights. Some people say he dodged a bullet leaving his Korean company, that there will be more opportunity here. Others say he's a traitor to his group. I don't believe either.

I think there's more to the story.

But—and I hate that there's a but—it's not my place. I'm just a girl. A week ago, I knew next to nothing about Kpop or Mpop or anything. There's no power I hold that can change anything that's happened to Woon, and getting involved would complicate my life and interfere with my studies.

Truth is, I'm helpless. And a bit of a coward.

"I can't stay here," I tell Blain. "Let's go back to the dorm."

Blain holds her lips together for a moment, unmoving. "I knew it," she says. "Are you really going to let him ruin something you've been dying to do?"

I bite down the urge to scream *yes*. "No," I say instead. "I already did the thing I wanted to.

We came here, didn't we? I already crossed it out. It's finished."

Blain releases a breath through puffed cheeks. "Fine. You need time. I get it."

Hard as Blain is on me, she does understand. She also lets me win when I need to. That's one of the reasons why I keep her around.

"Can we try one more thing on our way home?" she asks, pointing at a line of rickshaws, the drivers holding onto their bike handles and offering cheap rides. It would be a short jaunt to the metro, but totally fun.

The rickshaws only hold one person per seat, but the two drivers we hire promise us they'll stay together.

It's a totally different perspective of the city. Wind in my hair, brisk air in my nose, and brightly lit buildings rushing past in a bumpy blur. It's exciting, terrifying, thrilling—everything you could ask for in a rush.

I'm transported to another world. One where I can slip the night and be someone who isn't so anxious. A person that's adored by the general population. A girl who's not afraid of herself.

We've stopped for traffic, something I wasn't sure would happen with the way my driver's been squeezing through the cars. Mopeds buzz by in the dozens, too. Trying to get a leg up on the congested streets.

It's already loud in the city, so when I hear a noise booming above the din I turn my head.

Market stands topple over, flyers bursting in the air. Someone's being chased, and there's a chorus of screams and bangs as a group of burly security guards follow their culprit, or victim, I'm not sure which.

"Quickly," I shout at the driver, not wanting to be caught in the chaos. The driver gets the hint and takes off into the river of traffic, but the mopeds ahead of us are moving slow with no cracks to get through.

I can't see Blain anymore, and I'm aware of being a lone girl in a big city at night. Not to mention, the people causing the commotion are probably gangsters.

The rickshaw driver sees a hole and takes it. I'm relived only long enough to see the reason for the gap. The person being chased is headed straight towards us.

"Faster!" I cry, but a bike can't out-do the cars, and the hole doesn't last long. Everyone is trying to avoid the fight, and in the process, they're pushing the bad guy next to us.

I've already made up a whole story about the situation in my head. The boy running towards me is a gambler in a hat. The men after him are looking to get their debts repaid. They're going to give anyone in their way a beating, too.

Should I flee or brace for impact? With how fast the guy is running my chances are probably better in my seat. I start bouncing my knee anyway in an attempt to relieve the tension. Finally, an alley opens up and the rickshaw driver dives for the space.

"Wait," the boy calls as we start to pass him.

I lean forward in my seat, turning around so I can catch a glimpse of the perpetrator. At first it's just because I want to keep his face in my mind as a reminder not to be like him. But what I see freezes me to my chair.

"Stop," I yell, trying to tap the rickshaw driver. I keep turning my head, trying to make sure my eyes aren't deceiving me.

"Stop!" I yell again, but it's not working.

This has to be the craziest thing I've ever done, but I can't just roll by, not now that I know what's happening.

I half stand in the rickshaw, causing it to tilt precariously. I lean my head out the side and scream. "Woon!"

My hand reaches for him as his eyes meet mine. It takes a second, but I know the instant recognition dawns. He pumps his legs harder, but the rickshaw is speeding up.

I feel so inadequate with my short arms, a wish for height pounding hard in my skull.

Woon's hand reaches too, but we don't touch. A moped screeches between us and the rickshaw driver pedals on, leaving Woon in the dust.

DODGING DANGER

▶▷▶

"Stop!" I yell for a third and final time, now in English.

The rickshaw driver must be used to foreigners riding in his cart because he listens.

Woon does a half jump/spin thingy to avoid the moped. One of the security guards is clipping at his heels.

I start to step out of the rickshaw thinking Woon is going to hop in my place, but the rickshaw driver has gotten off his bike and is yelling at me and asking for payment. I turn my attention away from Woon, reaching for the Yuan in my necklace wallet. Before I can pull it out, the rickshaw starts to move, throwing me into the back of the carriage.

Woon is driving the rickshaw. *Woon* is driving the rickshaw.

I repeat the words in my brain one more time, but they don't sink in. No matter which way I look at it, I can't put the puzzle together. Woon might be Maximus, but for a major pop star, he sure seems like he's in trouble.

The traffic pools and drips forward like getting the last bit of honey out of a bottle. Not good enough for escaping.

One of the security guards—the giant of the group—grabs onto the back of the rickshaw, pulling at a chunk of my hair. No way. My hair is my best feature. He's going to pay for that. He's not getting Woon either.

My teeth sink into the stranger's arm, hard as I can go. Never in my life have I been this brave, but I really want to know what's going on here. I can't do that without Woon.

The guy lets go, jumping back with surprise and awe. There's an advantage to looking like an innocent girl. No one expects you to fight.

"That was the coolest thing anyone's done for me!" Woon yells as he glances back at me.

My chest swells, but the battle's not over yet. I watch the other guards with narrowed eyes. "Less talking, more pedaling!" I respond.

Woon makes a tight turn and my back stretches out of the open cart. I grab tight to one of the bars, catching myself. The rickshaw is thrown off-balance by my weight, the bar creaking under my grip.

I don't have a lot in the strength department, but this is life or death, and the adrenaline is at its highest point. I swing my body forward until we're swaying the other direction. The cart tips back and forth until we're righted.

One glace behind me shows a smoking car accident and a guard hopping over a bent hood. Wow, Woon has guts. I'm kinda swooning even though it's still scary.

The last guard has some serious stamina, and he's charging like a mad rhino out of hell. Woon's going way faster, but I have no idea where we are and I'm afraid this alley we're in is going to end.

A chicken flies past my face as an old lady screams and jumps back. "Sorry!" I yell.

I'm rocketed forward as Woon comes to an abrupt stop. I risk glancing ahead and gulp. Worse than a dead end, all that's in front of us is a set of stairs.

"Hold on!" Woon cries, and I panic.

Nah-uh. I've done some crazy things, but I can't handle this. "Maybe I should just get out!"

"I'm sorry," Woon says, "but they'll take you hostage."

I grip the bars tight and close my eyes, my knees to my chest. My teeth tear through my lip as a scream escapes at the first bump. This is not okay. We're going to die. I'm giving up my life for Woon, and I barely know him.

There's a moment when I'm pretty sure we're flying. The rickshaw crashes as the bumping starts again. A perpetual shriek rips from my throat. Another flight, more bumps, and one last race through the air until we're safe on flat ground again.

I look behind me to see what happened and find the stairs in disarray. A couple of people are sprawled out over pavement, a bag of rice spilled across the stone. The security guard is clutching his shin, a red river running out from under his pant leg. We've lost them all.

We turn a corner and all the adrenaline drains from my veins. I don't know if we're out of danger or not, but I can't handle anymore.

Everything that happened in the last ten minutes processes in my brain, and I have to swallow down the terror. What did I do? The whole of China is probably looking for him now.

"S-s-stop." I need to breathe.

Woon parks the rickshaw and climbs off the bike. He stretches his back then leans forward, hands on his knees. His breath comes out in rasps and he coughs a few times.

"We...need...to... leave," he says.

His hands slip off his knees as his ankles buckle. I jump out of the rickshaw as he falls to the ground. "Woon!"

I don't know what to do. I can't carry him. I can't even try to pull him up because my arms feel like jelly.

He tries to stand again but I press my palm to his chest to steady him. Holy mother, I'm touching his chest. I whip my hand back like I just got burned.

"I'll get us some help," I say, half standing.

He touches my leg. "No!"

I suck my hurt lip, my fingers gripping and un-gripping nervous-fast. I can't leave him here.

His hand trails off the side of my pant leg. "Give me a second. I'll be fine."

I start bouncing my foot. What if there are more guards around the corner? We're both dead if that's the case.

The sound of dirt scraping brings my attention back to Woon. He supports himself against a building with one hand, and brushes himself off with other.

"I should explain what just happened," he says, craning his neck until our eyes meet.

His beauty hits me hard in the gut. Perfect swoopy hair peeking out from under his cap. Coal-lined eyes. Leather pants. I think he was just about to perform. The hat must've come later.

I search his eyes, rove his face, my gaze lingering on his lips a second too long. It's not my place.

"That would be a good idea," I say, trying not to look at him.

I study the pattern in the brick for half a second before my attention returns to him. It's hard not to look at him when we're right here.

His perfect eyes are downcast, ashamed. He reminds me of a puppy that's been kicked. I can't believe I've gotten myself tangled up in this.

He meets my gaze, and a smile tugs at my mouth. I didn't ask it to come, but looking at him gets my happy vibes going.

He breathes a laugh, his head shaking. "Come on, we need to leave. It won't be safe for long."

"Lead the way," I say.

He doesn't budge. One shaking hand rubs his neck as he studies the ground. "Actually, I don't have anywhere to go."

Oh. Right. He'll probably get caught if he goes anywhere familiar.

"We could go back to my dorm."

I didn't think that sentence all the way through before it burst out of my mouth. I was just remembering Blain's back there and probably worried sick for me. And it's safe.

"Um," I say raising my hand in a stop motion. "Don't think anything weird. I mean, Blain is there and I doubt they'll—"

"It's okay," he says. "It's a good idea."

A little pink rises on the tops of his cheeks. Great, he's embarrassed for me.

I stuff a wad of cash under the bike seat, hoping the rickshaw driver finds it and that it's enough to cover the damage we did. We walk side by side until we get to a main road and hail a cab. Woon keeps his hat down while I do all the talking.

We're silent on the ride back to the dorm, both of us exhausted from our adventure. One thing's for sure, if it wasn't for Woon I wouldn't have known what a true adrenaline rush feels like.

I don't call Blain before we get there. My phone is dead anyway, because it's a crappy model. This is better. I know she'll yell at me, so I'd rather wait until she can see what an awful mess I am.

I've caught sight of myself a couple of times in the cabbie's rearview mirror, and it ain't pretty. I'm surprised my camera survived the melee. There's no reason to fix it though, Woon has already seen the worst of it.

He's a little beaten up as well. There's a scratch on his chin that has dried blood stuck to it. Chicken feathers are sticking out of his shirt, dirt on his shoulder. Somehow that just makes me like him more.

Pull yourself together, Jenica. You're going to be hurt otherwise.

"It's not much," I say as we walk to the gate outside my dorm.

It's not really a gate; it's a door in a cement block entryway. But since that door leads to another door, it acts like a gate more than anything else. There's graffiti on the concrete exterior and the once-white brick on the building is covered with a thin sheen of pollution.

Every apartment building in the city looks like this. Thank goodness the inside is nicer than the outside. It might be small, but it's clean. We have a living room, kitchen, bathroom, and one bedroom. The kitchen/living room area is tin-can sized compared to my parent's house back in the states, but the light wood floors throughout brighten the room.

Blain and I have done what we can to make it a home. We started a wall of all the pictures I've taken, mostly of tourist stuff and us being silly. There's a bonsai tree Blain's been caring for, and a few other cheap trinkets we bought off the streets.

"Wow," Woon says as he enters. "This is nice."

I scoff. "You're joking, right?"

He nods his head as he walks around, picking up a plastic Buddha I got from a street vendor. "This is way better than the dorm I lived in with my members when my group debuted."

I scrunch my brow. There are seven boys in his group. If I'm understanding what he's saying, he lived in a place smaller than this when his group was starting out.

I'm not sure what to make of that so I accept the compliment. "Thanks. I guess."

Awkward silence fills the small space between us, and I start looking around hoping Blain will pop out at any moment. Maybe I should've found a way to call her first.

I point to the bedroom. "I'm going to plug in my phone so you can use it. You should take a seat."

"Wait," he says, as I make for the door. He takes off his cap and fluffs his hair. "Can I just…I wanted to say…I mean…"

For someone who performs in front of huge crowds he's sure being shy. I thought I was the one with that problem.

"You can tell me," I say, putting my back against the wall next to my bedroom door. "I haven't blabbed to the media yet, have I?"

He laughs, shaking his head. "That's what scares me. You might be the only person I can trust in the whole world."

I frown. It's not funny. No one should feel like that.

"When I saw you in that rickshaw," he continues, his gaze on the floor. "You have no idea the hope you gave me."

He raises his eyes to mine, paralyzing me. "You trusted me without knowing who I was. You saved me when the media has done nothing but slander my name. You brought me to safety even though it put you in danger."

It wasn't anything spectacular. Just one human helping out another.

"Basically," he continues, looking back at his shoes. "I'm trying to say thank you."

I stand straight, wishing I could run over and hug him. How unloved has he been that he would say those things to me?

"You're welcome," I answer, unsure of what else there is to say.

He points a thumb over his shoulder to the couch. "I'll just–"

I nod. "Sure. And I'll just–" I say pointing to my bedroom.

It takes an incredible amount of energy not to shut the door on him too fast. My heart is beating triple time, fingers shaking.

You're welcome? That's really all I could think of? He poured his heart out to me and I acted like it was a business transaction.

I try to ignore my own stupidity, searching for my charger next to my bed. It's gotten twisted on one of the legs, and it takes me a second to unravel it and get my phone juiced.

My hand is on the doorknob when I hear a bloodcurdling scream come from the other room.

I rush out to see Blain with her hand over her heart, breathing heavily. She takes her purse and whacks Woon on the back with it.

"Don't scare me like that!" she says, adding a few more swings.

Woon is holding his arms over his head, shielding himself from her blows. "What did I do?"

I jump between them, pushing Blain back. She tackle-hugs me, sobbing into my shoulder.

Woon catches my eye and I shrug, not sure what's going on.

"I thought you were dead," Blain says between sniffles. "I lost you out there and your phone wasn't working, and then there was stranger in our house and I thought he was going to murder me."

Maybe I'm a bad friend, but I can't help but laugh. I thought Woon was a murderer when I first met him, too. Must be his height and his extreme manliness. I'm glad she was so worried about me. I was starting to worry about her.

"I'm fine," I say between giggles. "And Woon didn't deserve that beating."

Blain lifts her head, giving Woon a death stare. "You," she says, letting go of me and walking toward him with her finger pointing at his chest.

He backs into the corner as she approaches. "Are you the reason I thought my best friend died?"

"I'm sorry," Woon says. "I didn't mean to. The second I recognized Jenica, I saw a way out."

Blain flexes her jaw. "That's no excuse."

Woon rubs his hands together, head bowed. "Forgive me. If I can use a phone, I'll leave."

"No," I shout, losing my senses for once.

I clap my hand over my mouth, holding my breath. Am I really that desperate to keep Woon here? It's stupid. Logically, there's no reason for me to want him around. My body reacted without my brain keeping up. I can't remember the last time I let myself do that.

"Sorry," I say. "I didn't mean to shout like that."

Half of Blain's mouth rises in a smile. "Jenica being impulsive? Never."

I bury my face in my hands.

"You can stay," I hear Blain say. "If Jenica wants you around, I can't argue."

I stare at her wide-eyed, relaxing my arms. Blain winks at me, and I know she did all that to protect me.

"Here," Blain says, reaching out her phone. "Use it, and then stick around."

Woon accepts the phone with two hands, bowing as he goes. "Thank you," he says, bowing two more times. "Thank you, thank you."

Blain gets my attention as Woon turns around. She widens her eyes and tips her chin at the bedroom behind us.

I don't want to go in there, I want to stay with Woon. I shake my head, but she stomps her foot.

Woon puts the phone to his ear, back still to us. I guess it wouldn't hurt to let him have a private conversation. I sigh so Blain knows I'm not happy, and lead the way to our room.

Blain shuts the door behind us and falls hard on her bed. "What happened?"

I pace the room, not able to contain my nerves. “It’s a bit of a blur, honestly. Woon was running, and I ran with him.”

“So, you brought him here?”

I try sitting on my bed. “What was I supposed to do?”

Blain shakes her head. “Your heart is too soft, but I like that about you.”

“Blain,” I whine, resting my forehead on my palms. “You need to help me. I don’t know what to do. I can’t kick him out now that he’s here, but what if he needs to stay?”

“Well,” she says, stretching her arms behind her and resting her weight on it. “I wouldn’t have let him in here in the first place. That CSTAR company is not to be messed with.”

I know it, too. I’ve done some research since that day on the Great Wall, and I found out that CSTAR talent gets abused. Long hours, no food, so many appearances they don’t get to sleep. It seems like they’re dealing in shady stuff too, though I can’t piece any of that together.

What I do know is people who try to leave them end up worse than when they began.

"But," Blain continues, pulling me out of my thoughts. "I'm not you, and you probably did the right thing."

I look up, studying her face. She's not joking.

"For now," Blain says, "we let him stay. But...he has to go at the first sign of trouble."

Discovering Woon

▶▷▶

"Go talk to him," Blain says, her voice weary. "I'm going to get ready for bed. Worrying over you has left me exhausted."

I snicker. She always has a delicate way of putting things.

If she's going to stay in here, then I'll be alone with Woon in a small room. Why does that feel dangerous?

He's a celebrity, I remind myself. There's no way he'd go for a girl like me. Nothing to be worried about. I take a deep breath and nudge the door open, and then close it softly behind me.

"Good news," Woon says when he sees me.

He takes a seat on our couch, setting Blain's phone down in front of him. There's no tension in his body, no confusion in his features. He's totally comfortable, so I should be too.

I chose the chair furthest from him, anyway.

There's a small coffee table between us and we're sitting diagonal from each other. He narrows his eyes for half a second before scooting over so we're directly across. My gaze flits to the floor, heat tickling behind my ears.

"I'm sorry," he says, and I catch his knees straightening in my peripheral. "I'm imposing, aren't I?"

I look up, mouth open. "What?"

"Now that I'm safe and I've made my phone call, I should go."

He starts to get up, but I latch onto his wrist. "Wait."

Why can't I just be a regular person who responds when they're spoken to? He must think Blain convinced me he has to go, when in reality, just the opposite happened.

"You don't need to leave yet." The words come out tiny, and for a moment I'm not sure he heard them.

He sits, and my gaze travels to his face. He's on the edge of the couch. I had launched forward when I grabbed for him. That leaves our faces closer than they should be. This coffee table is much too small.

"Sorry," I say, removing my hand from his like it's scalding.

"You keep apologizing," he says, not moving from his position.

When I look at him again his eyebrows are down, mouth thin. His eyes are so clear, brown stained glass with sunlight beaming through. Common sense tells me to turn away, but I'm swallowed up in his gaze.

"Don't," he finishes in a whisper.

My tongue has turned to metal. I have to say something or he might run away again, but speaking is harder than I remember it being.

"Habit," I say, the word breathy.

He chews on his bottom lip, his dimple popping out with the movement of his jaw.

This isn't real. He's too beautiful to be concrete. What if he wasn't a superstar? What if we had met in a coffee shop like regular people? What if I wasn't terrified of him?

I clear my throat and scoot back, breaking the stare. He hangs his head, one of his hands rubbing the other fist.

"Goodnight!" Blain calls to us walking from the bathroom to the bedroom and giving us a wave. I don't think she heard any of that with the water running.

"Night!" Woon and I say in sync.

She shuts the bedroom door and I can hear the fan going. She really wants us to be alone. Probably so I can get over Woon.

"You were telling me some good news?" I ask, trying to swim through the awkward.

He doesn't look at me as his head bobs yes. "I have a way to get back to Korea."

My heart drops to my stomach. "Oh? That's fantastic."

I hope he buys my words, because I sure don't. He's still not looking at me, and there's a stabbing pain in my chest

"Yeah. It is," he says, reaffirming it to himself.

Crap. He's leaving, and I screwed up our friendship. If I really want him around, I need to act like I can handle that instead of being weird around him.

It's wrong of me to crave him the way I do. I'm keeping him for totally selfish purposes, and I know it. Even with that knowledge, I can't stop myself. It's like Blain is whispering in my ear to quit being such a prude and let myself feel for once.

I've spent two weeks trying not think of him, and I've done nothing but. This is as much as we can be, and yet, I have to see it through. If he leaves now, I'll spend forever dwelling on the time we had. I need him around so I can get him out of my system.

"When do you go?" I ask, my heart cracking.

He lifts his head, his face squinting. "I was going to ask you about that, actually."

I sit up straighter. "What?"

Woon rubs his hands on his thighs. "You see, my groupmate can't get away right now with management watching him so close. I need to stick around until tomorrow night."

"Oh," I say again, trying not to sound triumphant, even though I feel it. "Of course."

The thinking part of me must be working again because I manage to keep myself from jumping in the air and shouting, "YES!"

"Are you sure?" he says with one brow raised.

I'm sure, but why wouldn't I be? I nod to confirm, and he gives me the full effect of his smile. It's dazzling.

"I don't want to put you at risk. You can kick me out any time. Say the word and I'm gone."

Never going to happen. I take a deep breath, feeling light. "Sounds good."

I love the way his eyes crinkle as he smiles. "Great."

He leans into the couch and I stretch my arms forward. I want to keep talking to him, but I really stink at conversation.

I point my thumbs behind me. "I should get ready for bed."

"Sure," he responds.

"And," I say, "I'll bring you a blanket."

He nods. "Whatever you have, I don't want to be an inconvenience."

If only he knew how much I like having him around.

I stand up to leave when I hear a rumble behind me. Flipping around, I find Woon stiff-backed with one hand on his stomach.

"Was that–?" I start, looking at his hand placement.

He cringes. "I might be a little hungry."

I throw my head back as I laugh. "You should've said something."

I'm not sure what we have lying around, but there is food. I start searching through the cabinets. "How does ramen sound?"

"Perfect."

I pull out a pot and get the water boiling. There's some green onion in the fridge and I chop it up to add to the water for flavoring.

"Can I help you with anything?"

I jump, spinning to see Woon right next to me.

My fingers are sprawled over my heart. "You scared me."

He smiles. "I keep doing that, don't I?"

I swallow. He is way too close.

"Yes," I say, busying myself by cracking an egg. I don't even know if he wants egg, but I have to do something.

He doesn't leave my personal bubble. "I'll try not to do that anymore."

I have to get myself together and talk.

"I'm sure you didn't mean to."

"No," he says, taking the egg bowl from my hand and whisking it. "I came over here because I couldn't let you make my food for me. Now move."

I stare at him with my mouth hanging open. His eyes travel to our two-person kitchen table then back to me. "Go, sit."

"But–" I say, reaching for the ramen packet.

He takes it before I can, and holds it to his chest like he's guarding it. His toe hits my foot as he gestures for me to sit again. "I can make ramen by myself. It's not hard."

I don't like it, but I take a seat anyway.

He opens my fridge and takes out hotdogs, cheese, and rice. "Your ramen was a good start," he says, chopping up the hotdog into pieces. "But this needs to be taken to the next level."

I roll my eyes, but don't argue. Hot dog in ramen sounds like the most disgusting thing I've ever heard of.

Now that the water's boiling, he throws in the noodles and seasoning. He warms the rice in the microwave, and adds the hotdogs with the egg into the ramen pot. The cheese goes in at the last minute.

Maybe it's a good thing he's cooking. I can take full advantage of his leather pants from here. I should probably get him something more comfortable to sleep in, but I'm a touch shorter than him and Blain is a touch skinnier. I'll have to get him something in the morning.

Snatching a hot pad from the wall, Woon uses it as the centerpiece for the ramen pot. Then he serves up two bowls of rice, with chopsticks.

"What's this?" I say, looking at the bowl he's placed before me.

"Dinner," he says matter-of-factly.

I press my lips together, looking at the ceiling. "I'm not hungry, and you didn't ask me."

"Seriously?" he says, "After what we just went through? You need food to help you recover."

I'm still reliving it, and it makes my stomach churn. Food is not a good idea right now.

He sighs, picking up his chopsticks. "You're shaking, you need to eat."

"No, I'm–" I start, but then I notice my trembling hands.

"Open up," he says.

I'm in the middle of a "Huh?" when hot noodles touch my tongue. I slurp, pulling in as much air as I can to tame the burning. Really ladylike. There's a bite of hotdog in there, and some cheese, too. It's actually amazing.

"Mmmmm," I say involuntarily.

"See," he says, using the same chopsticks and reaching into the same pot. I guess he's not worried about my germs. "You need nourishment. Now eat your rice."

Might as well resign myself since he won't let it go.

I take a big bite and chew slowly, memories of home flooding me with the taste. I swear this rice is better than when I made it earlier, but I have no idea how he did it.

"More water," he says.

I look up, confused.

He then points to my rice. "It needed more water, so I added some before microwaving."

I squeeze my eyes shut, and then open them again. How did he read my mind?

He dips a spoon into the ramen broth and takes a sip. "I cooked for all my bandmates."

Uncanny. I wasn't going to ask him how he knew so much about food, and yet he answered the question before I could ask.

"Of course," he says, continuing the one-sided conversation. "I mostly just made ramen, but I'm dang good at it."

So crazy. I was just wondering if he could make anything else this good. Now I want to test him. If we really are on the same wavelength, maybe he can read what I'm thinking right now. I narrow my eyes at him and think as hard as I can, asking him the question in my heart.

Would you stay as long as I asked?

He has to leave, and I know it. But this is the first time we've sat down together and I want to get to know him more. If he leaves tomorrow night, it'll be a repeat of the pain I experienced the first time we separated.

I watch him eat for a few minutes. He keeps looking at me, but not saying anything. I really want to know if he can crack my question.

"Eat," he finally says around a mouthful of food.

I pick up my chopsticks and try some more of his ramen. So much for that.

"What?" he finally says after we eat in silence for a while.

I shake my head. "Nothing."

"No," he says, putting his elbows on the table and locking his fingers. "Not nothing. You want to ask me something."

Some ramen broth goes down the wrong tube, and I start coughing. How did he know? Maybe he didn't get it exactly right, but he knew I was thinking of a question.

I take a sip of water and clear my throat. "That's insane."

He raises his eyebrows. "What is?"

I smirk. "The way you can read my mind."

My face instantly flames up. I cannot believe I just said that.

He laughs, and I can't help but look at him. "So I was right?" he says through the laughter. "I was just guessing."

I don't want to laugh with him, but his face is so happy I can't help but join in. Just another check on the list of reasons why he's not real.

"So ask me," he says, his smile still wide.

"Oh no," I respond, shaking my head. "I can't. Too embarrassing."

He tilts his head. "Now I have to know."

"Nope." I shovel more food into my mouth to prove my point.

"Come on," he says, poking my arm.

I flinch away from his touch, feeling it all the way up my spine. So not fair. He's totally comfortable while I'm a wreck.

"So..." I say, needing a subject change. "You told me you'd explain what was happening downtown."

He scratches his head, and then studies his hands. "My career is a bit of a mess right now."

Okkkayyy... I don't think he has any idea how much I've been researching him.

"I think I know," I tell him. "This is just a guess based on what I've read online, but you're under a terrible CSTAR contract and you want out."

He's still looking at his hands, and I watch as his chest fills with air then collapses. "I wish it was that easy," he says. "If it was just the contract I could hire a lawyer, but what can I do when I've been kidnapped?"

My muscles go rigid. No wonder he's been running. I wish the people of the internet knew so they'd stop talking bad about him.

His fists are flexing hard, and I decide to listen instead of respond so he can say what he needs to.

"My future is over," he finally says. "My company in Korea will never take me back."

"What?" I ask, confused by the strong statement.

He grips the table, shaking the pot enough for drops of liquid to splatter around us. "I didn't have a choice. They stole me away from my company, forced me to sign at gunpoint, and then sued to get out of my previous contract."

I slowly sit forward, feeling more on edge than I was during the chase earlier. "What are you going to do about it?"

He looks at me, and I can see the tears pooling there. "I don't know," he says, inhaling roughly. "But I have to get back to Korea to figure it out."

Opening Up

▶▷▶

The revelation weighs on my shoulders. I have no idea what to say. If Woon has to go, he has to.

I pick at the side of the tabletop where something is stuck to the surface. I'd rather not look at him and let him know how I feel.

"Unless," he says, causing me to focus on him again. He shakes his head and looks away. "It's a long shot."

"No," I say. "You can't start something, and then not finish it."

"Why not?" he asks, "You just did it to me."

Oh, he's good. But this is different. "Yeah, well, my question didn't have sway on the rest of my life."

After I say the words, I realize it's a lie. Whether or not he stays is totally something that affects my future. Either I get over him, or he leaves me wondering my whole life. I need to figure out why I can't forget him.

"All right," he says, and I can see he's dying to tell me. Why else wouldn't he keep up the fight? "But you can say no."

I lean on my forearms, eager for more. "Spill."

"There's a way for CSTAR to leave me alone, but I can't do it myself."

I wait for him to say more, but he's looking at me like I'm going to straight up reject him without hearing the proposition. "What is it?"

The corner of his mouth lifts, just a smidge. "There's a video. It has everything I need to prove my innocence back in Korea, but I can't get to it because it's inside CSTAR."

Whoa. That sounds really dangerous. I'm not sure I'm the right person for dangerous. The rickshaw incident was one thing—I didn't have much of a choice. But willingly walking into the lion's den? Yeah, not sure I'm up for that. Still, I'm curious.

My eyebrows raise. "What are you proposing?"

He copies my position and lowers his voice. “Promise me you'll say no if it's too crazy.”

I already think it's too crazy, and I haven't even heard the plan yet. “Okay.”

“You go in and get it for me,” he says, cringing a little.

I already gathered as much. “How?”

He laces his fingers together as he sits up, almost like he's about to pray. “You could go in and audition?”

I shake my head to make sure my ears are clear. “Excuse me?

“Every Tuesday, they have an open audition. You could go in.”

This is absurd. “You want me to go in, and what? Pretend I can sing?”

He rubs the palm of his hands over his eyes. “Forget it. I knew it was a long shot.”

I hold in a sigh. It's not like I already said no, I just want to understand better. Even if I'm not the right person, I should still try and support him as much as possible.

“This means a lot to you, doesn't it?” I ask.

He glances at the tabletop, and then back up at me. “You know you’re the first person to ask me that. Everyone assumes I’m in this business for the fame, but I’m doing it because I love it.”

The conviction in his voice is tangible. I finally understand. Being a singer is more than a job for him, it’s his reason for existing.

“What would I have to do?” I ask, hardly believing what I’m saying.

“You wouldn’t have to sing,” he says. “All you have to do is get inside, and then I can guide you to it.”

I start to hyperventilate as I picture it. “Won’t I get caught the second they hear how bad I am?”

He laughs. “You’re not the first person who can’t sing who went to those auditions.”

I glance at the clock. It’s very late, and my tummy is full. That leaves my mind muddled. “I’ll think about it,” I say, even though it kills me. I should jump at this, but I can’t get over my own fears. Then again, if I say yes, he might stick around for a bit.

He stands up and takes my bowl. "Good choice. I'd be worried if you said yes right away."

Whoa. I'm glad I stopped myself.

He turns on the water and starts to rinse out the bowls. At first I think he's going to leave it at that, until he pulls out the soap.

"You don't have to do that," I say, standing up. "You made the food."

I try to reach into the sink when I realize that would require me to be shoulder to shoulder with him.

He turns off the water and shakes off his hands. "I'm your guest, and I have to pull my weight."

After he dries his hands on the towel, he places them on my upper arms. He steers me to the couch and sits me down. "You stay here and talk to me."

How can I say no?

The water is loud, but I can still hear him as he speaks across the room. "So tell me, Jenica, what's your last name?

I grab a pillow and hold onto it, folding my legs crisscross. "Why do you want to know that?" I ask, attempting to flirt.

"Come on," he says. "I'm sure you already know my birthday, my height, and my favorite color. This is the age of the internet."

I do know, but I'm not going to tell him that. It's amazing what I can find out about him online. He doesn't have the same luxury.

"Lee," I say, giving in. The most boring last name on the planet.

"Jenica Lee," he says, like he's testing it out. "Jenica Lee," he says again, his pitch going up. "Jenica. Lee."

I hide part of my face behind the pillow. "Will you please stop?"

He cranes his neck around to see me. "No. I like your name. Jenica, Jenica Lee."

"Uggghhhh."

He turns off the water and comes to sit next to me. "I'm sorry. I'll stop saying your name, Jenica Lee."

I whack him with the pillow. He laughs, trying to dodge out of the way but failing.

"Tell me," he says, turning my direction and folding his legs the same way mine are. "What's your deepest secret?"

I whack him with the pillow again.

"Hey," he cries, holding up his hands in defense. "I'm serious here. I should know everything about my host."

I face him and blow out my cheeks. "What you see is what you get."

Woon gives me a cocky smile, but it doesn't thin out his full lips. "I see a girl who's a mystery."

"What?" I ask, incredulous.

"I can't figure you out," he says, his voice quiet. "At the Great Wall, you didn't know who I was but you still tried to help me. Then even after you had plenty of time to read about what everyone thinks of me, you didn't hesitate to call out when you saw my face."

He hangs his head, hands fidgeting. "I can't believe I'm going to admit this, but you're the first person in a long time who's seen me as a person instead of a celebrity."

I scoff, shaking my head. "You don't have to say those things because I'm helping you. I know who I am, and it's not anything great."

"I don't think you do," he says, point blank.

My thermostat must be broken because it feels insufferably hot. I don't know what he's looking at, but it can't be me.

I need a change of subject, ASAP. "What were you doing on the Great Wall that day, anyway?"

"CSTAR didn't trust me to stay at the company without them, so they dragged me to where their rookies were performing," he says, relaxing into the couch. "It wasn't the first time I ran. In fact, I've been caged up like an animal until tonight. They let me go on stage to perform, thinking I wouldn't dare jump into the crowd, but I did. Then again, it wouldn't have worked if I didn't run into you."

Why does that make me proud? I didn't do anything, except bite a dude's hand.

"You know what, Jenica Lee?" Woon says, bumping me with his elbow. "I think you're good for me."

I whack him with the pillow one last time for being smart.

Something is pounding. Like a jackhammer or something. My eyes flutter, and the pounding gets worse with the light.

I groan, trying to shift position, but there's something heavy on my lap. My eyes fly wide open to see Woon lying on my legs, dead asleep. Turns out the pounding was my heart.

From what I can gather, we've been like this for a while. Woon and I were talking so late into the night, I don't remember going to bed.

Also, I'm pretty sure I was feeling up Woon's chest just now. Not sure how that happened.

I try to un-trap a leg only to find tingling pain shooting up my thigh. Sat on it too long.

Woon stirs, his forehead crinkling as he sits up. "Jenica," he says, even though he has yet to open his eyes.

"It's about time," Blain cuts in.

We both whip our heads around to see Blain standing in the kitchen, some bags on the table.

"I bought you some new clothes, Woon," she continues, like she didn't just catch us snuggling. "I suggest you both shower because you stink."

I try to smell myself, but it doesn't seem too bad.

Blain starts to stomp off then comes back. "And shower separately, please."

My face is a million degrees. How can she even say such a thing?

"You can shower first," I say to Woon, running into the bedroom after Blain. He looks bewildered, but I don't dwell on it.

"What the crap?" I ask, the moment the door is shut.

Blain looks me up and down. "You know you're on the verge of having a boyfriend, right?"

She cannot be serious. "He's a celebrity," I whisper through clenched teeth.

Blain busts up laughing as loud as she can. "Honey, if he doesn't like you, then I'm boring."

I slow my breathing as I study her. She's dyed her hair fuchsia today, and her nose ring is a flat silver sun. She's wearing a black top with a dark purple tulle skirt that sticks out all directions. Her pumps have to be at least five inches, even though she's already tall. They're also covered in glitter. Boring is the last thing Blain is, and she knows it.

"But–" I start. The argument dies on my lips before I have the chance to continue.

Blain has her hands on her hips, head cocked to one side. "Think about it. If he didn't like you, he wouldn't have fallen asleep on you like that."

Yes, but why would he like me? He did say some nice stuff last night, but that was because he was grateful. Besides, he's leaving.

"Look," Blain says, swiping open her phone. She's about to pull up the internet when I grab her phone from her and lock it again. When I open it back up, there's a new picture there.

"What is this?"

Blain is usually tough as nails. I've seen people call her all sorts of things. I've watched heads turn everywhere she walks. Strangers have approached her and asked her all kinds of weird questions. She doesn't get embarrassed.

I look at her again, making sure I'm picking up the right cues. Her face is the color of a tomato, and she's not making direct eye contact. She always makes eye contact.

"This is someone in Woon's group, isn't it?" I say, pointing to the screen.

She tries to swipe it back from me, but I adjust so I can study the picture closer. The letters G.O. are written in cutesy font with hearts around it.

"His name is Go?" I laugh.

"No," she says, grabbing the phone from me. "No more than Woon's name is Maximus. Besides, it's pronounced G. O."

Oh, she's delusional. "You like him." It's not a question.

"You like Woon!" she shouts.

I rush to cover her mouth. "He's in the other room."

She rips my hand away. "Listen," Blain says, "The shower is running."

I pause, listening, and hear she's right. I suppose we're safe to talk.

"So," Blain says, "you're admitting it."

My arms fold as I *harrumph*. "I am not." Because I don't have a shot with him.

Blain taps my shoulder. "What were you doing last night, then?"

I tap her back. "Talking."

She wiggles her eyebrows. "Didn't look like talking to me."

This time I give her a gentle shove. "Shut up and quit changing the subject. We're talking about you liking G.O."

"His name," she says, "is Hyungsoo, and no we're not. We're talking about you and Woon getting together."

"Hyungsoo? Really?"

Blain swipes open her phone again and pulls up a browser. "Look. A Woon is known for his cold personality. Even when the other guys are being warm, he stays back. He wouldn't talk with just anyone."

I crinkle my brow, not sure what to think.

Blain changes the site. "There's even a bunch of fanfiction about him being rude to someone before falling in love."

"Wait," I say, still teasing her. "Fanfictions?"

I snatch her phone from her and notice something she's reading. "G.O.'s ideal type is a girl who's conservative." I read aloud. "Are you seriously getting into this?"

Blain huffs, taking her phone back. "You're the one who started this. I was researching Woon for your sake, and I ended up getting a little sucked in."

My eyes widen as I see right through her. She's one of them. Those girls who are totally gaga over K-pop. Hyungsoo, or G.O., has totally held her captive.

"How many fanfics have you read?"

I didn't think the red on her face could deepen, but it does. "A few."

"A few?" I question, shaking my head. "I was wondering why you were on your phone so late every night."

"They're good, okay?" she says. "And yes, I'm a fan now, so you'll just have to get used to it. Heck, plenty of people like football and superheroes, why can't I like this?"

Wow, she's defensive. I'll have to remember not to cross her. And honestly, I like it too. I've spent more time this past week researching Woon than worrying about my homework, which is saying something.

"Crap!" I shout. "I have homework to do!"

"You're really going to–" Blain says, but I don't listen to the rest.

I charge out of my room with the intention of getting my book bag from the coat closet, but I run into something hard and wet the moment I open the door.

My lips collide with bare skin. There are only two other people in this apartment, and one of them is behind me.

Cleared Air

▶▷▶

I step back, the flesh on my lips sticking a little as I do. I've just run into Woon's perfectly arched collarbone. How can I look into his face?

This did not happen. I'm going to pretend it didn't happen.

He's not moving, and I can only imagine what he's thinking. I'm going to have to apologize. It's one thing to see pictures online, it's another to feel his body warmth and smell the soap he just showered with.

He has a towel draped over his shoulder, sweat pants covering his lower half. Either Blain knew his size, or Woon looks good in anything. I'm guessing it's the latter.

I force my eyes to travel from his perfectly sculpted chest up to his face. What I find there isn't what I was expecting. He has a wicked grin and an evil gleam in his eyes.

Forgetting all about my apology, I shove him. "What are you doing standing outside a girl's room?"

Shoving was a mistake, because now I've felt his exposed abs. Geeze, he might as well call me a perv.

I close my eyes and ball my fists, backing up.

"Maybe you should get dressed," I hear Blain say behind me. "There's one more thing Jenica and I need to discuss."

"Wait," he calls, and I open my eyes to see he's still smiling. "I couldn't find a shirt."

Blain starts looking around her. "Are you sure..." She grabs a plastic bag off her bed and riffles inside. "Sorry about that," she says, shoving the shirt in his grip and the door in his face.

I don't remember sitting, but here I am, sunk into my bed. I'm awkward enough without accidently kissing his chest. Holy crap, I kissed his chest! I might die from embarrassment.

Blain shakes me. "Get yourself together, Woman!"

"You were right," I say, my breathing short and fast. "I shouldn't have let him stay. This is very bad."

"No," Blain says, pulling me to my feet. "It's not."

I collapse on her. "Yes, it is. Did you see his face? He thinks I'm totally inept. Maybe I am."

Blain pulls me off her and moves her head so I'm forced to see her face. "You're the smartest girl I know, and it's his fault for listening outside our door without knocking."

Was he really listening to us? What did I say? I start for the door, but Blain grabs my shirt and wheels me around until I'm sitting on the bed again. "Calm down, okay? We're not done talking."

I'm sand falling through an hourglass. No matter how I wish I could turn myself around, I can't. Gravity has complete hold, making it impossible to change what just happened.

"Will you wake up?" Blain says right in front of me.

I fall into my pillow wishing I could scream, but knowing Woon would hear me.

"It's going to be fine," Blain coos, rubbing my back. "Why don't you forget about your homework and get ready instead? I bought us lunch already, so you don't have to worry about cooking."

Lunch? I didn't think I had slept that late. I pick up my phone and gasp. It's already three. How did I not notice when I was looking at Blain's picture earlier?

"All right," Blain amends. "An early dinner."

"But he's coming tonight," I say, butterflies flaring up.

Blain juts her chin forward. "Who's coming tonight?"

I lie down again, this time on my back. "I don't know. One of Woon's groupmates."

"Members," Blain corrects. She's gone from red to completely pale.

"You don't think..." I say, wondering if it's this G.O. person.

She shrugs. "There are five other guys besides those two. What are the chances?"

"One in six," I say.

Blain runs her hands through her hair. "Those are good odds."

I have to stop panicking and start acting. If another member of his group is almost here, I don't have much time left. Woon wants me to help him, and I still haven't agreed. If I do, does that mean he gets to stay until Tuesday? And if he stays, what does that mean for me? Am I going to put my studying on hold and ruin my semester abroad?

There are too many questions without answers.

"I'm going to shower," I say. "You keep Woon occupied, and don't let him go anywhere."

Blain barely acknowledges, still a zombie on my bed.

I want to get ready fast so I can have more time with Woon, but I also want to look hot. If that's possible. I decide to skip washing my hair so I don't have to blow-dry. Thank goodness for dry shampoo.

Curling is a must, however, as is makeup. I keep glancing at the time, trying to make myself go faster, but beauty is a process. I pick out my favorite graphic tee and my skinniest jeans, topping off the look with my black Converse.

When I emerge, the T.V. is on. Blain is totally unfocused, but Woon is laughing his head off. There's a scattering of orange peels around him and I notice he's gone through half a bowl of Mandarins.

Blain must've bought his shirt too small, because I can't unsee what's underneath. Did she have to get white?

This is going to be okay. We're both adults, and we both have voices. We can work this out.

"Hey," I say to Woon, trying to act cool by leaning against the wall. Instead, I miss the wall by half an inch and stumble forward. I stand straight and clear my throat, shoving my thumbs in my back pockets. “Whatcha doin’?”

Woon glances at me and drops his orange. It rolls under the coffee table, but he doesn’t bother to pick it up. He clears his throat, his focus turning back to the T.V., then to me, then back to the T.V.

He closes his eyes and shakes his head. “Um,” he says, blinking rapidly. “I’m just watching this show.”

His back is stiff, hands on his knees. Do I really look that bad?

“Oh good,” Blain says. “You’re out of the bathroom.”

I’ve never seen her so out-of-it. She nudges me as she passes by to enter the bathroom, totally unaware of what she’s doing.

“What’s with her?” I say, taking her place on the couch next to Woon.

Woon steadies his breathing, still not looking my direction. “I don’t know.”

Dang, that chest kiss was probably the worst thing that could’ve happened. Woon is leaving soon, and now he won't even talk to me. Maybe it's good. I can get over him faster.

I stand and make my way to the kitchen, bending over to look in the fridge. I'm starving. "Hey," I call. "Blain said she bought some food, do you know–?"

My words fall short when I turn around to look at Woon. He eyes are wide. Was he looking at my backside? He quickly pulls his knees up to his chest and buries his face like that will hide him.

"Never mind," I say turning back around. "I'll find it."

There's an unopened take-out box on the counter, noodles inside. I flip it open and find the chopsticks, shoving the drawer closed with my hip.

My gaze falls on Woon, who's back to playing the part of a two-by-four. The orange he dropped is still under the table. It doesn't look like he's enjoying his show, so I'm not sure why he's still watching it.

I turn my back to him and try to forget it. Curse my shyness, or else I'd think of something to say. I eat the noodles quickly hoping it will calm the nerves in my tummy.

The only reason I can see for acting this way is because he's leaving. Maybe last night some of the energy from the chase was still in him, but now that he's rested and cleaned up, he's come to his senses enough to realize he never should've associated with a pion like me.

Accidently kissing his chest was the cherry on top of the weirdo sundae.

I have to fix it. It's not in my personality to confront, but this is a desperate time.

I slam down my chopsticks and spin around. "Look," I say, drawing his attention to me. "I didn't mean to do that. Don't think I meant anything by it."

He's still not making eye contact with me, his gaze somewhere above my head. "I have no idea what you're talking about."

Great, do I have to spell it out? I plop on the couch next to him, hugging the same pillow I did last night. I can see his breathing speed up as I sit. His eyes are darting around until they land on the T.V. again.

My fingernail digs into the button on the remote as I turn it off. There, now he has to pay attention to me.

"I didn't mean to kiss you, or to touch your abs," I say, the words strained. "I'm sorry."

His Adam's apple moves up and down his neck as he swallows. His fingers are tapping his knees now, and he still won't turn my way. "It's fine," he says, but his sincerity is lacking.

"Look," I say, "I know you're way out of my league. Honestly, I wasn't trying to make a move on you."

He blinks, looking at me for the first time. "What are you talking about?"

"You know, that...incident." I move my hands as I speak as if that will make the point clear.

"And what incident is that?"

Now he's just playing with me.

"I mean," I start, scratching my head. Since he's not going to get it unless I'm direct, I might as well be honest. "It's not like I don't enjoy flirting with you, but I didn't mean to kiss your chest."

"Hold up," he says, looking like he's holding back a laugh. "What did you say?"

He should know he doesn't have to pretend for me. "You're a big shot celebrity, and I'm a nobody so you're not talking to me because of everything that's hap—"

The pillow rips as he tears it from my grip. He leans over me so I'm forced to lie down, one veined arm planted on the edge of the couch and the other over my head.

Holy mother. Does he not know how dangerous this is? He's not touching me anywhere, but he might as well be running his hands over me for the trouble he's causing. Every part of my system is on high alert—blood pumping, nerves rippling, breath coming out short.

All I can focus on are his perfect plump lips and his strong jaw. He dips down, his face so close I can taste the oranges he was just eating.

"Whoa," Blain says from somewhere near the hall.

I slide out from under Woon, my cheeks burning.

He sits up like nothing happened. I swear if this is a joke.

Blain laughs. "Guess I can't leave you two unattended anymore."

I shoot her a death glare. She has no idea what just happened. I don't even know myself. It's all so confusing.

I'm about to get mad at her when I notice her appearance. She's wearing a baseball cap over the purplish part of her hair, only exposing the blonde underneath. I don't think I've seen her in ordinary jeans, and wait, is that...a cardigan?

There has to be an explanation for this. I didn't know Blain had these things in her wardrobe.

I try to prod by making faces and hoping she guesses my thoughts, but she crosses her arms and shakes her head like now isn't the time. I want to drag her back to our room so we can talk, but at that moment the doorbell rings.

My gaze instantly lands on Woon. The only person we're expecting is the other member of his group. My time is up, and I've done nothing with it.

"I'll get that," Blain says, putting on her fakest smile.

Woon still won't look at me, and I have no idea what to say to him anymore. So, I ignore him, following Blain to the door. She looks through the peep-hole, and then straightens her sweater and adjusts her cap.

Blain's appearance is suddenly explained. It must be G.O. behind that door. That fanfic really got to her. No wonder she was so dazed when I entered the living room.

The doorbell rings again, and I see Blain's hand hesitating on the knob.

A body presses into my back; Woon's leaning over me to open the door. Does he have no sense of personal space? As if I wasn't already dizzy.

It takes all my effort to focus on the person beyond the door, but I do. I barely see G.O.'s face when I hear him say, "We need to go, I've been followed."

The Chase

Woon pulls G.O. inside, shutting and locking the door. "What do you mean you've been followed?"

Now that I see him in person, I can understand why Blain thinks he's cute. He's got huge doe-like eyes and thick black hair. But...he's only as tall as her shoulder, and she's wearing sneakers. I don't like it.

G.O. whips off his hat and runs a jittery hand through his hair. "A fan spotted me at the airport and posted online. It didn't take them long to track me."

Woon picks up the bag holding his old clothes, and ties it tight. "What are we waiting for then? We need to go."

No. He can't. I'm not ready.

"It's not that simple," G.O. says, popping his cap back on before I get the chance to form an argument. "CSTAR is going to have this place marked, which means these girls are in trouble."

Crap. Because I took Woon in, I'm a target. We'll have to see this through together. At least we don't have to part ways yet.

G.O.'s eyes rest on Blain for a second, and he gives her a half smile.

Her knee twitches like it's about to collapse, one of her shoulders slumping. I've never seen Blain with hearts in her eyes before, and it's a little unnerving.

"We have to move," G.O. continues, setting down Woon's bag and tugging him towards the hall. "I assume you two can come until all is clear?"

"YES!" Blain screams, reaching for her messenger bag.

G.O. raises an eyebrow. "Okay, then. Let's go."

I decide to grab my wallet and phone, stuffing them in my back pockets before we go.

Blain starts heading downstairs, but G.O. whistles to her before she can get far. He points up instead, still dragging Woon behind him.

I shrug when Blain looks at me. I hope this means he has a plan.

Our dorm is located on the third floor, which means we have two stories to climb in order to reach the top. I have no idea what's waiting there. After everything I've gone through with Woon I half expect a helicopter to be above the peaked roof with its rope-ladder unfurled.

I try to catch Woon's gaze, but he doesn't look backward. G.O. has let go of his wrist, but Woon still holds it forward like he's being dragged. G.O. opens the attic stairs and gestures for us to climb up.

Blain goes first, opening a door to the roof. Cold wind sweeps in, tossing strands of black hair in my face.

The three people in front of me run out without hesitation, but I pause at the top of the ladder. What am I doing? I don't want Woon to leave, but if I follow him now, will I be able to come back?

As much as I want to be around Woon, school is first. Saturday is almost gone, and I still have loads of homework to do. Skipping one class was something, but abandoning everything?

"Jenica?" Woon has his fingers on my arm, his eyes looking golden in the late afternoon sun.

"I don't know if I can do this," I say, being honest.

Woon's hand feels so warm on my skin. He's starting to get a light stubble on his chin and it's sexy. I'm torn between what I'm leaving, and what might be in front of me if I follow Woon.

"Guys!" Blain calls, looking over the edge of the building.

I want to see what she's pointing at, but if I leave this doorway, there's no going back.

"Not good," I hear G.O. say.

Woon takes my hand and squeezes, sending fireworks through my nervous system. "Stay here," he says as if he knows what's going on inside me. Maybe he does.

He barely leaves my side, peeking over the edge before running back to me.

“CSTAR’s thugs are invading the building right now. If we don’t move, it’s over.”

I’m not left with a choice then. I leave the comfort of the doorway and embark into whatever crazy thing we’re going to do next.

“Come on,” G.O. shouts, running to the far edge, the one that connects to the building next to us.

“Are you serious?” I say, teetering on top of the sloped roof. I don’t know how G.O. was able to run on this thin piece.

There are five buildings in a row, each the same height with the same number of apartments in them. Between them there’s a gap the length of my forearm. They’re close together, but not close enough. There’s no way he’s thinking of jumping, is he?

Before I can think it through, Blain who is in front, jumps first and keeps going.

“Wait!” I hear someone say in Mandarin behind me.

The CSTAR thugs have made it to the roof. There's no more time to think. I'm still quaking when I feel Woon's hand in mine.

"We can jump together," he says as I look at him.

I nod because there's no time to answer. I run without looking, leaping on Woon's blind faith. My knees bend as I land, but I don't stumble, thanks to Woon's grip.

We start running again, and he doesn't let me go.

Blain and G.O. are a building ahead of us, and we have to sprint to catch up. It's not fair for me because Blain has longer legs, and G.O. dances as much as Woon does—I'm the only non-athlete here. There's no way I'll be able to keep up, but I push harder because I know I'm being chased.

We run all the way to building five, where Blain is holding the roof door open for us. She slams it shut when we're all through, crawling in behind us. Woon lets go of my hand to help barricade the door. I take the lead down the stairs, but everyone is close on my heels. As I'm reaching for the front door, Woon spins me around.

"You don't have to come," he says, his words rushed.

"What?" I'm not able to process because the chase still has my blood pumping.

"I can go out there and create a diversion," he says. "They'll follow me and leave you alone. You can go back to your apartment. They won't bother you if they know where I am."

I shake my head. This isn't how I wanted to say goodbye. I've made it this far, I'm committed.

G.O. brushes past us. "No time to talk now, kids, idiots on our heels."

"I'm sorry," Woon says. He takes my hand again, holding it tight.

He has nothing to be sorry for. His brows furrow, and there's something I'm reading in his face I can't quite pin down. Regret?

There's no time to process, because we're running again and Woon's back is to me.

Woon's hand in mine is the only thing pushing me down this street, and even then I'm not sure how much longer I can do this.

"Jenica," Woon says, stopping abruptly. "I will find you. I don't know when, but I will."

My voice comes out pinched. "What are you–?"

He cuts me off by kissing my sweaty forehead. "And I'm not too good for you."

Did he just–? What is–? There's no time to process. He can't go. Wherever he runs, I'll follow. If only he wasn't ten times faster than me.

My fingers stretch into the open space between us, swimming through the air in an attempt to grab onto Woon's shirt. Footfalls thunder behind me as Woon bolts to keep up with G.O. I don't see Blain anywhere, but I'm sure she's somewhere.

I'm winded, achy, and cramped, but I pour every last bit of energy I have into a final sprint after Woon.

G.O. knocks someone from their moped and climbs on.

"No!" I scream, as he pulls Woon on almost in the same motion.

"Stop!" I try again, and Woon turns his head to look at me, his brows pulled together like he's in pain.

G.O. kicks off just as Woon's eyes widen. He's shouting something in my direction, but I don't hear him.

Rough hands drag me away. I kick and scream, trying not to lose sight of Woon. But he's gone, and my hands are being cuffed behind my back with cold steel. I'm so out of breath, but the fight is still there. I do everything I can to free myself from the men in suits who are wrestling me into an awaiting van.

He said they wouldn't take me, but he was wrong.

Hope drains from me as they shut me in. Woon is gone. CSTAR has me. I put my forehead to the window, searching for Blain, but she's not where I last saw her on the curb. Maybe they put her in a different car? I cry out for her until my throat bleeds.

Someone puts a cloth over my mouth and the world around me fades in shimmering distortion until I don't see anything at all.

Kidnapped Jenica

▶▷▶

Everything hurts. My eyes sting, my neck has a crick, and my muscles are sore. I don't remember why I fell asleep in a dance studio. The bright wood floor and the wall of mirrors aren't clicking together in my head.

I try to rub my eyes, but my hands are cuffed so tight my shoulders scream in protest. That's when the whole messy scene rushes back to me. CSTAR invading my dorm, Woon riding away. Not seeing Blain before I blacked out.

My feet clamor for purchase on the slippery floor, but my ankles are tied too. My mouth isn't covered, for now. Screaming will probably just get tape put over my mouth anyway.

I'm alone. There are two sets of doors, and I'm guessing guards are sitting outside each one. They wouldn't just leave me with a way to escape. Not that I could with these restraints.

I'm not sure what CSTAR plans to accomplish with one girl of no big importance. It's not like Woon would come running after me. I'm just someone who happened to be at the wrong place at the wrong time. Three times.

I struggle, and struggle, and struggle with the ropes around my feet, but it's no use. Those scenes in movies where people wiggle until the knots come loose are such a joke. Either the bad guy is too dumb to know what a real knot is, or the victim is triple jointed. Neither of those scenarios apply to me.

My body slips to the ground until I'm lying on my side. I'm so tightly bound, I can't even get myself to a sitting position. I have to think. This can't be the end.

There's not much I can do until they untie me, but I have to be fed at some point, right? Oh gosh, what if I need to go to the bathroom?

I'm betting there are people outside the doors, but I need to be sure. "Hello?" I call. "Is anyone out there?"

I hold still while I listen. There are murmuring voices behind one of the doors. I wait for a few minutes to see if they're going to open up, but nothing happens.

"Excuse me," I say, a little louder this time. "I really need to pee!"

I'm hoping they'll cut me loose if I complain enough. Maybe I can do one of those calmly-walk-to-the-bathroom-then-make-my-escape things. How cool would that be? I just need to learn martial arts in the next minute without the use of my limbs. I know, it's a done deal.

The door opens, thank goodness, and a handsome older gentleman in a baby blue floral fitted suit enters. His shoes look really expensive.

"Why did you tie her up?" he says, exasperated.

Does that mean I'm going to be let go?

He bends down next to me and loosens my legs first, and then opens the handcuffs, being gentle as he does so. "I'm so sorry," he says in a sweet, coaxing tone. "The idiots out there keep thinking this is an action film."

I spread my feet apart, and he helps me sit up, letting me take a minute to catch my breath and rub my sore wrists. This is the time when I should pull out a gut kick and twist his arm until his shoulder bone cracks, but I can't. The instinct to defend myself isn't there if he's not fighting. I can't find my urge to run when he's being nice.

"I can't apologize enough," he continues. "When this is all over, I'll get you a relaxing massage so your body can feel better."

A massage would do me good about now.

"You must be thirsty," he continues, pulling me to standing. "I heard they put you to sleep too." He shakes his head. "I'll get you anything you want. Is there a food you've been dying to try?"

I guess I'm a little hungry, but I can't seem to find my voice. I wish I knew what happened to Woon, G.O., and Blain.

"Forget it," he says, linking our elbows to steady me. "I'll just order a little of everything."

We head through the door and I see the guard who captured me standing at attention.

"Idiot," the person holding my elbow says, gently hitting the guard dude in the back of the head. "You don't treat our guest this way."

The guard bows, the whole top of his body bent over. "I apologize, President. Forgive me."

President? Like the president of CSTAR? It can't be this guy, he's too kind. He raises his hand like he might hit the guard again, but he doesn't. "Be careful next time."

Now I'm really confused. What kind of company is this? The mob? This boss person doesn't seem that mean, but he obviously employs thugs. Especially if they're the same people who followed us before.

"Did you need to use the restroom?" he asks me as we pass some stalls.

He's just going to let me go in there, alone? Seems pointless to run when no one is holding me back. I decide to go into the bathroom just to test my theory. That, and I need to pee a little.

Sure enough, I'm in there alone. I spot a little window that I could probably climb through, but it's high up and I bet it would hurt to squeeze in such a teeny space. Not to mention I'm feeling faint from my time tied up. Woon wanted me to get that video, and he thought I could do it calmly. Fighting will be pointless unless I know what I'm up against, anyway.

Until I've assessed the situation, I'm going to stick around and absorb as much information as possible.

Morning light filters in through the glass. I must've been knocked out through the night.

"Feeling better?" the CSTAR president says to me as I come out.

I nod. "I'm a little worried though."

He takes my arm again and pushes a button to the elevator. "What seems to be the problem?"

"I think my friends are looking for me," I say, just to see what his reaction will be.

He pats my hand. "Of course. I've already contacted Woon, Hyungsoo, and Blain, if that's what you're worried about."

Maybe they are coming for me. We get in an elevator, which means we won't be walking by any exits. He pushes the top button and waves his badge in front of a little sensor thing. It's only the fourth floor, but I sense it's going to be fancy.

Sure enough, the second the doors open, I gasp. It's obviously an office, but it's a cleverly disguised office. The first thing that grabs my eye is the pool table in the middle of the main sitting area.

There's a huge kitchen to my right, and a massive window on the back wall looking out over the city.

The desk is set up on a platform at the back of the room, opposite a baby grand. If it weren't for the three monitors and stacks of paper on the desk surface, I wouldn't believe any work occurred here.

President guy releases my arm and opens the giant fridge. "Would you like something to drink?"

Every kind of soda, sports drink, and energy booster I could want is stacked inside the door. There's alcohol too, but I'm still a minor.

"W-w-water's fine," I stutter. My throat is pretty dry, and I need the hydration.

He puts the water in a fancy glass and hands it to me. "Again, Ms. Lee, I apologize about your treatment. I do hope you'll take a seat while I make a phone call?"

He pushes a button on the coffee table and a giant flat-screen TV appears above the fireplace. He plops the remote into my hands and he gives me a generous smile. "Your food should be here soon."

Why is he being so cordial if I'm a captive? It's making me really confused. I'm not sure what else to do. I know I'm still a prisoner, but this isn't really a jail sentence. I'm still worried about everyone, but he's making it seem like everything's okay. Or maybe my judgment is impaired because I'm hungry and dizzy from being knocked out.

"Thank you..." I'm not sure what his name is.

"Please, call me Chet."

Weird name for someone who's Chinese, but I'm not going to say anything. "Thank you, Chet."

I turn on the TV. Not because I'm interested in watching anything, but I can tell Chet wants his conversation to be private.

It's already on the nature channel when I click it on, so I settle in to watch a cheetah hunt.

"What?!" Chet screams.

Holy mother sheep. I was not expecting him to explode like that. He's been so cordial until this moment. I pretend I don't notice the outburst

"Get him up here, right now," he says through clenched teeth.

I change the channel to a random show as he hangs up the phone. He's pacing over by his desk, timing his breathing. I really need to get out of here.

There's a knock on the door. I shift in my seat, wondering if this will be my only opportunity for escape. Now that I've had some water, I think I could handle finding that video.

Chet strides past me to let the person in. I'm not sure I could fend off Chet and squeeze through, but I should at least try.

I stand, inching my way closer to the door, trying to remain unseen. Chet turns the knob and a wave of good smells slam into me.

One glance at the cart holding the food, and I have to close my mouth to keep from drooling. Meat, dumplings, fruit, eggs, rice, and a few things I can't identify come rolling in.

Focus. I have to get out. I can't worry about the delectable food in front of me. I have to keep my attention on my goal.

I sneak closer, risking a glance into the hallway behind me. That's when I spot him.

Woon, head down, being escorted by two guards. They bring him through the door with the food. Like he's just another dish on the menu.

I can't see all of Woon's face, but his body posture tells me what I need to know. He thinks he's been beat.

"Jenica, come on over," Chet says, waving to me.

I try to catch Woon's gaze, but he won't look at me.

I shuffle my feet, unsure of my next move. Do I play along, or start to show my defiance? My rebellion needs to be timed right, or else I'll just end up bound and gagged back in the dance studio. I have to think. I must be smarter than them.

As I approach Chet, he puts an arm around my shoulder. Gross. It takes almost super-human restraint to not pick up his hand and drop it off me.

I want to call out for Woon, but he looks so hurt I don't know what to do. I try to step out of Chet's arm, but he locks his fingers into my shoulder—hard. Leaving isn't going to be as easy as I'd hoped.

"Please, sit," Chet says to Woon. The guards lead him over to a couch, but Woon doesn't bend to sit. His focus is straight ahead, to a blank space on the wall. Jaw clamped and eyes narrowed.

The girl with the cart pushes a button, and the pool table turns over and rises to the height of a regular table, which is pretty cool. I wonder what other secrets this office holds.

Chet guides me back to my chair in front of the TV, diagonal to Woon, and flips the screen off. "You're not going to say hello to Jenica?"

I press my lips together and try to look as small as possible. Woon doesn't turn his head my way.

"Would you like something to drink?" Chet says to Woon.

Woon stands, shoulders back, defiance written on his locked jaw and squared shoulders. Maybe he's not defeated yet.

"Tea," Chet says, standing. "Nothing loosens people up like tea. Please, sit."

This time it's a command. The guards on either side of Woon push him down to the couch. Woon shoves their hands off him and sits forward, back straight with hands on his knees.

Chet comes back to the sitting area with some plates. "Jenica, what would you like? Steak? Rice? Pot stickers? Chicken? I bought it all for you."

The food looks and smells really good, but my hunger is not as important as this situation. "I lost my appetite," I say.

Chet laughs, piling food on a plate anyway and putting it on the table in front of me. I don't touch it.

"There has to be something you like," Chet coaxes. He sits next to me, picking up some chopsticks. He roves my plate, until he snaps up a dumpling and holds it next to my mouth.

Now I'm worried that it's poisoned or something if he's forcing me to eat.

Chet pushes the warm sticky wrapper against my lips. "Say ahh."

Woon stands up, and the guards mirror his movements. He reaches across the table and grabs my good wrist, jerking me away and knocking the plate to the floor. In one swift motion, I find myself squished between Woon and one of the guards. Woon puts an arm around my shoulder and holds me close to him, or away from the guard, I'm not sure which.

Chet puts his elbows on the table, chin cupped in his palms. "So she does mean something?"

To Woon? No. He's just being a gentleman. Trying to keep me safe from the bad men.

"She's innocent in this," he says.

Chet is looking at his nails, picking at a cuticle. "I think you know what has to be done here. I'm not treating her poorly."

Woon's grip on my arm tightens. I'm a little afraid of what's going through his head. "You're still holding her against her will."

Chet laughs, slumping into his chair. "I think we already went over that when you first came here. You already signed the contract. All you have to do is keep making money. I don't see anyone losing in this situation."

Obviously, Chet doesn't think kidnapping is a crime since he's done it more than once now. We have to get that video and free Woon.

Woon is massaging my arm, gripping and un-gripping as his hand moves up and down. I don't think he knows what that does to me. Herds of butterflies are taking flight in my belly.

"Enough," I say, finding the courage to speak up.

Woon looks at me, nostrils flared. I know he doesn't want me in the middle of this, but I can't stand here and watch any longer.

"Woon's not working for you anymore," I say. "What you did isn't legal."

Half of Chet's mouth slowly raises in a smile. "I think it is. It's been holding up in a court of law, anyway."

I narrow my eyes at him. "We will find a way out of this."

"Jenica," Woon says, his voice next to my ear. "You don't have to defend me."

Don't I? If nothing else, Woon is my friend. I need to be here for him.

"Back on that rooftop," I say, "I made the choice to leave everything behind and run with you. How I got here isn't important. I'm answering the question you asked me over ramen, and the answer is yes."

I might not be walking into an audition and sleuthing my way to the video, but that doesn't mean I can't help him.

Woon nods his head, and then keeps nodding like he's convincing himself that nodding is the right thing to do.

"If you let her go," he says, turning to Chet. "I won't fight anymore."

What the crap? I just told him I'd help. I don't understand why he's doing this.

Chet stands, a satisfied smile on his face. "I knew you'd come around."

He makes eye contact with me, and I'm truly afraid. Something was not right with that look. It was more than just a triumphant stare. There was something evil in his eyes.

All right, so maybe that's a little dramatic, but there's a really dark feeling in the pit of my stomach when I think about it.

"Let's make it official then," Chet says, clapping his hands together. He goes to his desk, leaving Woon and me alone with the guards.

Woon turns to me, holding onto my arms and looking me up and down. "Are you really okay? Did they hurt you?"

"I'm fine," I say. Except for the whole knocked-out-and-tied-up thing, but he doesn't need to know those details.

Woon pulls me in for a sudden hug, and I stiffen. "I tried to get you out," he says. "I'm sorry I failed."

Half of me wants to push him away. Tell him to snap out of it and fight for his chance to go back to Korea. The other half of me wants to lean into his hug, put my arms around him and tell him we'll find another way later. But there is no other way, and I know it.

Woon pulls back to search my eyes, but I don't know what to say. He can't give up his career to save me. I'm not worth it.

Chet comes over with a single pen in his hand. It has some buttons on the side, and his thumb hovers over one of them. "If you promise into the microphone," he says, putting the pen between Woon and me so Woon can speak into it.

Woon flexes his jaw, and I try to silently beg him not to do it. I can't handle the sorrow in his eyes.

He takes the pen from Chet's hand and pushes the record button. I feel like I'm being ripped apart, but I don't know what to do to stop this.

"I, Nam Woon, promise I will be true to the CSTAR contract as long as Jenica Lee is safely returned to her apartment and left alone for the remainder of her life."

My fists ball at my sides, teeth grinding together. How could he do that so casually? I was going to figure this out. I didn't know how, but if he had given me more time.

Chet swipes the pen back. "You know this is in your best interest. You'll make a lot more money—"

"I don't care about the money," Woon snaps.

Whoa, that's the first time I've heard him raise his voice. He has to be dying inside right now, and it's because I couldn't run fast enough. I feel like I'm shrinking into the floor and I'll disappear if this keeps being the reality.

Woon, still facing me, takes my hands in his. "Will you let me take her back?"

I stare in Woon's perfect deep brown eyes, wishing this wasn't happening.

"Don't think so," Chet says.

Woon turns his gaze to Chet.

"According to your contract," Chet continues. "Your training is still in session and will last for three months, or however long the contractor sees fit."

The words all go through my brain, but none of them absorb. If he's in training, why wouldn't he be able to leave?

Woon grips my hands tighter but doesn't look at me.

"Part of training," Chet says in a business-like tone, "is that you can't go anywhere without my say. I can look up the exact wording if you'd like me to."

"Please," Woon says, closing his eyes. "This is the last thing I'll ask for."

Chet puts his thumb and forefinger on his chin, looking up at the ceiling. "Hm...how about *no*."

With a wave of Chet's hand, I'm being ripped from Woon's grip. He tries to hang onto me, but he's being dragged away as well. My mind swirls through the possibilities of getting out, but there's a road block in my brain and I'm stuck. My legs won't even listen to me, and I trip as they shove me into the elevator.

If I made the decision to fight, why am I letting this happen? There's no plan, no hope. If I elbow these two big guys and push another button on the elevator, can I get out? I try looking at the one next to me, but he's probably six-foot tall and there's also a bandage on his hand where I bit him. Crap, I doubt he'll give in that easily.

I try to backpedal as they pull me into the lobby, but it's no use. I'm just a weak girl who can't save the guy she likes. In fact, I compounded his problem.

Hot, dust-filled air slams into me as the doors open. I have to squint my eyes against the high sun. The guards throw me to the ground, and I twist my still tender ankle.

Pain vibrates through my bones, opening my almost healed injury afresh. Woon said I saved him, but it was the opposite. If it wasn't for him, I never would've made it home after that day on the Great Wall. He was the one who drove the rickshaw to free himself from danger. I was the one who hesitated when CSTAR came after him, too.

He's a complete prisoner, shackled to CSTAR forever because of me. If we had never crossed paths that day, he might have found a way back to Korea to sort it all out. Instead, he can't do anything without Chet's say.

I try to put my feet under me, forget the hurt and push my way back to Woon, but the sting is too much. I end up on the pavement once more. Strangers weave their way around me, staring down at the disheveled mess of a person on the ground.

That's all I am. A pile of crap who was too stupid to help Woon when he needed me the most. Why did I have to realize it a second too late? Woon kissed my forehead, didn't he? He told me he wasn't too good for me.

Yet, I suppressed that and pretended like I was nothing more than a piece of chewed-up gum. That's not what he thinks of me. If it was, he wouldn't have sacrificed his one passion for me.

I'm so blind. All this time he's been pouring his heart out to me. He even tried to stop noticing me the last time we were together in my apartment, but I didn't see it. As far as Woon is concerned, I haven't seen anything clearly.

He likes me, and I returned that affection by abandoning him.

Pounding Fists

▶▷▶

I can't just leave. Who knows where the strength comes from, but I stand and ignore the throbbing in my foot. I shuffle my way to the door and try the handle, but it's locked.

"Hello?" I call. I have to get in there. Woon has to know how much I care for him.

I raise my hand and give the glass a rap. "Hello?"

Woon's face is centered in my brain, swelling until my head might explode with thoughts of him. I bang harder. "Hello!"

A girl with a bun at the top of her head walks by, and I rap on the glass faster. "Hello, hello!"

She gives me one stink-eyed look and hurries away.

"Let me in!" I call, but she's gone.

I stay at the door, face pressed to the glass for what feels like hours. My fist has found a methodical rhythm, and I *pound, pound, pound*, only speeding up when people walk through the lobby. Each knock is an apology. I'm such an idiot.

"Miss," someone says behind me. I turn around to see two police officers.

"Thank goodness," I say running toward them. "My friend is in there against his will and I need to—"

"Riiiight," one officer says, talking over me. "I'm sure your *friend* will get your fan mail. Why don't you come with us, and we'll get you home nice and safe."

Is he saying he doesn't believe me? "There's been a misunderstanding," I say with a laugh. "You see, I really am friends with Woon."

The cops exchange disbelieving looks. Crap. I already know how this is going to play out. I've been kidnapped enough to know when someone's going to apprehend me before I get a chance to state my case.

I give the officers a bow. "Have a nice day."

Then I run. I've had no food and only a little water. Combine that with a sore ankle and, well, it only takes a few strides before each cop has a tight hold on me. They drag me to their car, but I don't go easily.

Why couldn't I have been raised as a ninja instead of a bookworm?

"You're not under arrest," the officer says. "We just need you to sit here until your guardian arrives."

They're still holding me without cause, like I've told them a million times since I was first shoved into the back of their car. I wonder how much Chet pays the police commissioner for this kind of service.

When I asked them what my crime was, they said it was stalking. Ha! Chet's the one who's been stalking Woon.

At least I know Blain is on the way. I called her with my one call, and luckily, they let me use my cell. She said she was able to avoid CSTAR, though I don't know how.

"Jenica!" Blain rushes in and hugs me. "Are you okay?"

"I'm fine," I lie. I just let Woon sign his life away. I don't think I'll be fine again.

Seeing Blain triggers everything I've been holding in. She looks as tired and ragged as I feel. She's been through a lot too. I have no idea how she got away after the guards came, but I'm glad she did or else I'd be alone here forever.

She really is the best, how could I lie to her? I cover my mouth and shake my head, begging the tears not to come.

Blain takes a seat next to me and strokes my hair. "It's okay," she says. "Everything's going to be fine."

I fall into her arms, and she squeezes me tight. "Why do I have to like him?" I say.

It wasn't like I was planning on falling so hard so fast. It hasn't even been enough time to know if it's real. Yet, we've made an impact on each other's lives. That's not something you can just wish away.

"I know, hon, but you can't help it."

I bury my head in her shoulder. "He recorded a verbal agreement for those people. I don't know if he'll ever get out."

Blain holds me at arm's length. "He did what?"

I shake my head. "Not here. Let's get back to the dorm first." I figure we'll be safe there. Even if CSTAR knows the location, they got what they wanted, and they're not coming after me again.

We're out of money, so we have to take the metro back to the dorm. I keep quiet as we wander the streets to the closest stop. I'm walking blind, half hoping someone tries to rob me so I have an excuse to be injured. All I want is to lie down and let the people trample me. It's all over. Woon is stuck at CSTAR with that twisted man. I can't believe I didn't fight him when I had the chance.

My eyes burn as I try to keep them open on the train. My stomach keeps reminding me I haven't eaten all day. I let it growl—it's the best punishment I can give myself.

Blain barely closes the door to our dorm when she pounces on me. "I want to know the whole story."

"Hang on," I say, because I need to gather my thoughts. I set down my phone and my wallet, taking a deep breath. "My plan," I start, voice cracking, "was to find the video showing Woon's forced signing. But that backfired because I stood there like I was incapable of humanity instead of helping him."

Blain guides me to the kitchen table. She plops me down in a chair and takes the seat opposite me. "You did nothing wrong. I ran away. I hid. I watched them drag you into that van and I did nothing. I'm your best friend, and I did nothing. It's normal to be afraid."

Tears well in my eyes, and I cover my face to sob. "But doing nothing cost Woon his career in Korea. I can never expect him to forgive me. I'm just a fling, but his career is his life. He'll have to work for that monster forever."

Blain bangs the table, startling me. "I stayed away because I figured I could do more for you from the outside. Form a plan at the very least. Now that we're together, we have an even greater chance of saving Woon."

It makes sense, but I'm not sure we can do anything. That was a live-in-the-moment sort of thing.

"Don't move," Blain says, standing. "You need nourishment if we're going to plan."

One corner of my mouth lifts even though I don't want it to. I hate that she can make me smile when I want to sulk.

"It's not much," she says, placing our re-heated takeout from the other day in front of me. Now that I think of it, this was the last thing I ate. It's been over twenty-four hours. I snarl down the noodles even though the oil has leaked out after being microwaved. There are only a few pieces of meat left, and I end up popping them in my mouth one after the other without fully chewing.

"Slow down," Blain says, her eyes huge.

For the first time I notice she's still in her conservative get-up. It's a new set of clothes, but still not Blain.

"Wait a second," I say, "is G.O.–"

Blain bites her lip, brows arched down. Crap, I know that look. That's best-friend speak for please-don't-be-mad-at-me.

"Is he here?" I whisper-yell.

Blain slowly nods, giving me big puppy-dog eyes like she's afraid I'll kick her.

"What?" I scream. "Why didn't you tell me?"

"Shhh," she hushes. "He sleeping."

So what? Woon is in danger.

Blain adjusts in her seat, picking at her fingernails. "There's one more thing."

I arch one brow, my patience thin.

"He's the one who dropped Woon off at CSTAR."

My jaw drops. Why would he do something so reckless? He had to know Woon would get in trouble. "What? Why?"

"Woon insisted," Blain says. "He told G.O. he would go by himself if he didn't do it. There was a fight..."

"Are you serious right now?" I ask, raising my voice. "Why didn't you tell me right away?"

"Jenica," Blain says, leveling with me. "You get really hangry. I couldn't talk about this without getting you some food first."

I laugh, because it's so utterly ridiculous but so true. Blain was right to feed me first.

"Anyway," Blain says, "G.O. was hurt. He has a cut on his arm. He only just got away. I brought him back here because I didn't know what else to do. Hopefully some rest will help."

"It's just a scratch." Blain and I turn our heads to see G.O. standing in the hallway. He's dressed in a pressed shirt and tailored slacks. Where on earth did he get those clothes? And his hair is all gelled up out of his face.

I sniff instinctively and notice he's put on cologne, too.

Blain stands, her hands fumbling. "Hyungsoo, I hope we didn't wake you."

"I've been awake for a while now." He smiles. "You actually came home right after I finished showering."

Blain's face goes bright pink. Was he trying to make her picture him in a towel?

"I see you found your suitcase," she says, gesturing to his outfit.

What is with this dynamic? There's so much tension in the room I feel like I'm being squeezed out of a tube. There's only enough room in here for Blain and G.O.

I stand as well, walking between the two so they break eye contact. That was an uncomfortably long staring situation.

"I believe we have a friend to save?" I say, because I know both of them have forgotten the real reason we're all together. I wonder how much they made-out while I was gone.

"Right," G.O. says, popping on a pair of sunglasses. "Let's go."

I scoff. I can't help it. He's being such a peacock right now. He didn't even have to display his bright feathers for Blain to fall. I wonder if he knows that, and he preened anyway. Probably.

"Wait," I say as Blain and G.O. head for the door. "We're not going in with a plan?"

G.O. smirks. "I'm the plan."

If I felt like a third wheel before, it's only compounded by Blain and G.O. squished together in the backseat of the taxi. I'm on the far left side with G.O. on the right and Blain between us.

G.O. offered to pay so he wouldn't get recognized on the streets. I keep hearing Blain snickering, all her attention on him. I have no idea why she's snickering, but I don't want to know.

We pull up to CSTAR headquarters, ready to walk right back into the mouth of the tiger. So far, all I know is G.O. is going to offer himself to get Woon out. Because that worked so well last time.

G.O. hands the cabbie some cash. "Stay here," he says to the two of us. "We need a getaway car."

Blain nods like she has no problem with that, but I'm not going to back down so easily. G.O. shuts his door and I open mine.

"Stay here," I say to Blain who reaches out for me when she sees me leaving.

I don't turn back to see if she follows. I think she'll listen to both G.O. and me. At least I hope. I hide behind my side of the cab while G.O. stands in front of the big glass doors without knocking. I hear a buzz, and he pushes open the metal plate to gain entry.

Taking off at a run, I hop up the steps and get my fingers between the open doors just in time. They pinch at my skin, and my ankle protests, but my need to save Woon is stronger than my own physical limitations. I'm sure my body will pay for it later, but the nervousness pumping through my veins dulls the pain.

I can't believe I made it back inside CSTAR. It's not winning, but it feels like a victory. G.O. takes the elevator, but there's no way I could wait calmly. I dash up the stairs to the fourth floor to get my butterflies out. I don't even know if they're still in Chet's office, but that's where instinct tells me to go.

Having made it to the top of the stairs, I take a second to compose myself before I stride to the door and push it open. It doesn't even stick. No doubt Chet is expecting me.

I'm panting, out of breath, feeling like I've run a marathon to get to this point. So when I see everyone, including G.O., sitting around having a civil conversation, I'm confused.

"Jenica," Chet says. "My prize. So glad you could join us."

My skin feels oily from the second he says my name. The setting looks casual, but something's not right. I can feel it in my bones.

Chet points to an open chair. "Please, have a seat."

I glance at Woon whose head is hanging. Even though I can't see his eyes, his head shakes. It's slight, but I feel like he's signaling me not to listen.

"No thanks," I say with a smile. "I'd rather stand."

My legs are trembling, but standing has its advantages in a fight.

"Have it your way," Chet says, turning his back on me.

G.O. twists in his seat and starts waving his hands, mouthing the word *go*.

Yeah, right. I just got here. I'm finally in the same room as Woon, and I'm not giving up that easily. I want to move to Woon's side, but when he lifts his head, I can tell he wants me to stay where I am. I don't know why, but I trust him.

There are dark circles under his eyes; he looks worse than I feel. Unless I look that bad too. In which case, we're even.

"You couldn't walk away, could you?" Chet says, arranging some papers. His tone of voice frightens me.

What exactly is going on here? The lights are dim, most of the illumination in the room coming from the busy city outside the large window.

Chet steps toward me. "It's good you're here," he continues, nodding. "Now I won't have to come looking for you."

I stumble back. Me? He wanted to find me? Why?

"You just thought you'd swoop in here and take Woon away?" Chet stops by a side table, his gaze narrowing.

Well, yes. Maybe he's under a verbal contract, but we can figure that out when we get out of China. I don't know when I realized that was the only way, but I'm going with him. Screw school–if Woon was willing to give up his career for me, this is the least I can do for him.

Woon is mouthing to me, begging me to run to the door. I don't want to abandon him, but the more Chet talks, the more I feel like something bad is about to happen to me. Maybe if I run, Chet will follow, leaving Woon free to escape.

Both G.O. and Woon are signaling to me now. That's when I notice the broken pen on the table. I'm not sure how that happened, but the verbal agreement is over, which makes me a target again. I take a step back, holding my arm out behind me. My fingers grab the knob just as a buzzing sound emanates from the door. Locked.

"Nice try," Chet says, a deranged smile on his face.

He's waving something in his hand. Probably the buzzer that locks the door.

"You can't leave," he says, "because I need you."

Me? What would he need me for? I'm just an average girl who happened to meet someone way out of my league. Someone who likes me too. I can't say he still will after this moment, but we had our chance.

The elevator dings, and a tall girl wearing a tight, short dress slinks out.

Chet claps his hands, that insane smile plastered on his cracked lips. “Now that we’re all here, the fun can start.”

I turn around and try the knob again. This seems like seriously bad news.

Fingers pinch my shoulders, a guard taking me away from the exit.

“Don’t make me force you,” Chet says. “If I can’t have Woon, he’ll just have to be ruined. Guess who’s going to help with that? You. We might as well ruin his little friend while he’s here too.”

I don’t want to turn around and look again because I can already guess what’s going to happen. This girl is selling her body for money. Creating a scandal big enough for headline material. The headline of the National Enquirer.

I might not know much about foreign pop culture, but I know that Asians are not forgiving of slander. Once a celebrity’s name is ruined, it’s ruined for good.

Video or not, it would be the perfect blackmail for CSTAR to keep Woon in their grip forever. I can't let it happen.

If I don't take action, this is the end of Woon's career, forever.

Standing Up

▶▷▶

I can't just stand here and let this guy take Woon and destroy him. Clinging to the doorknob isn't going to do me any good. I made the mistake of not taking action once, I will not do it again.

The elevator must still be working because model-girl just walked out of it. All I need is to distract Chet long enough to get out. Which seems impossible. I have to try anyway.

"Ruin, huh?" I say, slowly turning around.

Bodyguard guy, the one with the bandaged hand again, is totally in my personal bubble. I want to throw up with him this close to me.

I narrow my eyes at Chet and lower my voice. "You can ruin him over my dead body."

I can't say I know much about self-defense. I've seen more action in the past two days than I ever expected to see in a lifetime. There's one thing I do know: all males have a soft spot—right between their legs. It's the first place men protect when they feel threatened.

My palm shoots up to the bottom of the bodyguard's chin first. He catches my wrist before I can do any real damage, but it doesn't matter—I only did that to distract him from my real goal.

I may have one hurt ankle, but my knee is working just fine. I put all the force I can to crunch his tender area.

He doubles over in pain, stumbling back.

I don't know what overcomes me, maybe I've watched too many action-themed music videos lately or maybe I'm just caught up in the moment, but I decide to throw in a kick to the chest for good measure.

The first thing I do is run to the elevator and hit the button. When I turn around I see Chet bent over in pain, no doubt hit by one of the boys. Woon and G.O. grapple with two other security guards. Woon has one of them by the hair and he pulls the dude's face down to his knee. I want to scream "Nice one!" but now's not the time.

The elevator dings, doors sliding open. Model chick has retreated to the corner, curled up against the wall. With Woon's man taken care of, G.O. and Woon gang up on the last guard.

"Guys!" I yell, facing the doors as I hold them open.

I twist my neck to see G.O. grab a guard and swing him around to face the far wall. Woon gives him a swift kick in the butt and G.O. lets go just in time so only the guard collides with the wall.

The elevator doors keep trying to close on me, but I don't care if I have to stand here all night. I'm getting these guys out.

Chet is starting to stand, stumbling in my direction.

"Woon, hurry!" I scream.

G.O. and Woon are jumping over the furniture trying to get to me in time, but Chet is closer. He grabs my shirt and tugs me back into the room, causing me to lose my grip on the elevator doors. They try to slip closed, but I keep my leg in the way.

Woon is there. He pulls Chet to his feet and punches him in the face.

G.O. falls into the elevator and pulls Woon in with him. I remove my leg and the elevator is on its way down.

We did it! We're free from Chet! I wrap my arms around Woon and he staggers into the side of the elevator. "I'm so sorry," I say, smashing my head into his chest.

For a second, he's stiff. His hands hang at his sides and his body goes rigid. I don't let go though, I'm never letting go.

It takes a second, but he melts. His fingers run along my back as he envelopes me in his embrace.

"I'm sorry too," Woon says. "I shouldn't have let Chet take you out."

I put a hand to his chest. "You don't have to say anything. I was the idiot for letting him."

"Um, guys," G.O. says, breaking up our little moment.

The second he speaks, the elevator jerks to a stop. Both Woon and I turn to see what G.O.'s looking at. A little screen has unfolded from the ceiling. It flickers on.

Chet's there, his mouth a straight line, his eyes serious. He holds up the same button he pushed to lock the door upstairs.

"Did you really think I wouldn't have control over my own elevator?"

My arms slip off Woon. Does this mean we're trapped?

"Since you're so stubborn about cooperating," Chet says, "I thought I'd throw in another little surprise."

The screen flickers again, and I recognize the dance room I was first held in. This time Blain is there, tied up in ropes much like I was. Only, she has a gag in her mouth.

"No," I breathe.

The screen twitches back to Chet. "Nice of you to leave a hostage sitting outside. You owe me a hefty cab fee when this is all over."

Not Blain. Anyone but Blain. She's my best friend, and she's innocent in all of this.

"I'll give you ten minutes to decide what you're going to do. Either Woon comes back upstairs and complies with my wishes, or your friend dies.

I'm not playing around anymore. It takes ten minutes for the engine to restart. Then your elevator is coming back up my office. See you then."

My knees give out. It's an impossible decision. If I let Woon upstairs, he lives a life of torture from the worst company on the planet. Chet will stop at nothing to keep Woon under his thumb. It's either that or I let my best friend die. Neither one is an option I'm willing to take.

"We have to get out," I say. "It's our only choice."

"And leave Blain?" G.O. argues.

"We can't do that," Woon agrees. "I'll go back upstairs."

I grip his shirt. "You can't just sacrifice the rest of your life for one moment. I let you do that before, and I can never forgive myself if you do it again."

"We're not letting that girl die," G.O. says. "Her life is more important."

Woon pulls me into another hug, and I can hear G.O. sigh. He must be feeling a lot like I did on our way here.

"Just let me do this for you," Woon says, whispering in my ear.

I push him away. The last thing I want is distance, but he has to understand.

"Listen to me," I say. "I can save her. You stay here and don't give into Chet's demands. I'm going after her. It'll all work out."

Woon runs his hands through his hair. "How are you going to do that with them watching you?"

Music video knowledge again, for the win. I point to the ceiling. "You're going to lift me up through there, and I'm going to climb to her. They may see me leave, but they won't be watching the elevator shaft."

"No," Woon says. "This elevator is going to start moving in a minute and you could get hurt."

"Woon," I say, grabbing his hands. "I want to be with you." I confess. I still don't know his feelings for sure, but I have to tell him mine. "I want be with you for as long as I can. If you give in to him, I'll never see you again. That would be death for me too." I whisper the last part, my heart aching.

I don't know what makes me do it. It must be all the courage swelling in my chest, but I stand on my tiptoes to reach Woon's lips. It's one quick kiss, but the meaning behind it is so much more. I'm committing myself to him, if only we can get out of this.

"If he won't lift you up," G.O. says, "I will. You've convinced me."

I smile, a blush creeping over my face.

"Plus, I don't want to watch you two kiss anymore," he adds.

Woon pulls me in for one last hug. "I trust you. Be safe."

I'd rather be smashed by an elevator than watch my friends suffer. If this is going to be the end, I'd say it's a good way to go.

Second Chances

▶▷▶

I know I'm running out of time. Chet will no doubt move the elevator the second the engines start up again. I bet he can't wait to crush me. He's no doubt enjoying this little game because he's a sick, twisted man.

I climb up a few rungs until I can no longer hear Woon and G.O.'s voices, and then I pull out my cellphone. The signal is weak, but it's there. I remember how CSTAR had the police on their side before, so I'm going to use that to my advantage.

120–Beijing's 911–rings three times before anyone picks up. "Please come quickly," I say. "A horde of crazy fans has broken into CSTAR Entertainment and they're holding hostages."

"Stay on the line," the operator says, but there's no way I'm going to do that. I have to save my friend.

I make sure she knows where CSTAR is, and then I tell her I'm breaking up and that the guys with guns are going to find me soon. Then I hang up. That should get someone over here, at least to investigate.

It hurts every time my ankle pushes on one of the bars but I climb through the pain. I can't go down, the elevator's in the way. I'll just have to sneak through the building—Chet's eyes on me—until I get to the basement. I'm not really sure what I'm going to do when I get there, but I'm prepared to fight.

The emergency elevator exit is covered in spider webs, and I can see little curls of rust coming out from under the bottom. Great. This is going to be a workout.

I heave at the door, but it won't budge. What I need is something to get underneath and pry open the slot. There's nothing loose around me, and I don't know how much longer I can stay on this ladder. I'll just have to use something I have on me, like my cell phone case.

It's not anything I really loved, just a simple plastic rectangle, but if I break off the raised edges, it should be able to scrape under the door.

Working as fast as I can, I pop off all four sides and start scratching. Below me I hear the sound of engines warming up. That's all the motivation I need. I don't care if I break my wrist holding on, I have to scratch faster.

My phone case breaks in two, but I brush it aside and keep working. This time, when I pull on the door it slides open. I climb through as the cables behind me start to move. Just as I draw my leg in, the elevator whooshes by, taking the man I love with it.

That's right–love. We've been through too much together to have it end on a lighter note. People don't give up their lives for each other if they're casually dating. The second Woon gave that verbal contract to save me, it transformed to so much more. I just didn't realize it until now.

I take the stairwell to the basement, glancing behind me as I go. I keep expecting a legion of guys in dark suits to descend upon me, but there's nothing. That makes me more nervous about what's to come. Then again, Woon and I have successfully injured a few people these past two days. Maybe Chet's out of goons to do his dirty work.

I get even more nervous when I get to the dance studio. It's still open. I untie Blain without a problem and give her a huge hug. Now we just need to get Woon back. All Blain and I have to do is exchange a look to be on the same page. No matter what, no giving up.

Just then, a giant screen flashes on in the room. What the crap? Does he have the whole place wired with screens? I'm not going to sit here and listen to more of his drivel. I drag Blain from the room and another TV flips on at the end of the hall.

I laugh to myself, thinking about the ending of the Wizard of Oz. Chet is the dude behind the curtain. He thinks he's God, but he's just a stumbling idiot with a few cool gadgets. I'm not going to let him get to me.

Chet's words are blaring through the speaker, but I don't listen. I just pull Blain up the staircase until we get to the main floor. There's a giant screen behind the front desk, and this time, the sound is so loud, there's no ignoring it.

"Stop!" Chet yells, and I do, but only because I know two things he doesn't know.

1. I spotted the police outside the door and they're sure to hear whatever he's saying. There's so many officers outside, not all of them can be corrupt. Two more TVs are on around me, blasting the sound. Everyone on the block is going to hear it.

2. My phone has a record feature that I make sure to turn on as soon as Chet starts talking.

"Go ahead, Chet," I cry, "tell me what you want."

"That's better," Chet says, his voice echoing around the building.

The camera pans around to Woon and G.O. Both of them have guns to their heads. That's why I was feeling so nervous. If I got through so easily, then surely Woon was in trouble.

"All the doors are locked, Princess. You're not getting out of here."

He thinks he's so clever, but he can only resort to violence. It's not going to win in this situation. I have to do this calmly. I can't afford for Woon to get hurt. Not now that I know my true feelings.

"Says who?" I shout. I'm not sure how well he can hear me, plus I want my phone to pick up every word. "I could break this glass right now."

The guy with the gun to Woon's head tightens his grip. "Then your boyfriend is going to die."

I can't let his words shake me. I have to be strong so people can know what a deranged freak they have on their hands. "Why would you kill the one voice your company can't live without? You've gone this far to get him. How many times have you kidnapped him?"

"The number's not important," Chet says.

"So you did kidnap him? You forced him to sign that contract too, just like you are now."

Chet pans the camera back to his evil little face. I can't believe I thought he was handsome when I first saw him. He's the ugliest person in the world.

"You know I did those things, but that's not what's important. Are you going to comply with me, or am I going to have to shoot him?" The camera swoops back to Woon. "Your choice."

I look behind me and see thc police standing at the door. Chet must be too absorbed in his game to notice law enforcement approaching the building.

They point to the door and hold up their sticks, asking if it's okay for them to break in. I nod.

"I hope you like life in prison," I answer, "because if you kill Woon, that's where you're headed."

"I won't let you win!" Chet screams, but it's too late.

Blain and I jump out of the way as the glass doors explode. The cops march in over the shattered pieces, and I hear helicopter blades hovering overhead.

G.O. and Woon tackle their gunmen at the same time and spin them around like it's an orchestrated dance. In fact, they both shrug their shoulders at the exact same moment and kick the guards while they hold their hands in the air—wrists bent. I have a feeling it's a dance they both know.

The gunmen are down, but G.O. keeps dancing. Chet is making a run at them, his camera shaking, just as the door gets knocked open,

S.W.A.T. teams piling in through the stairwell and the roof. They're safe. Blain's not dead, and no contract is going to hold up in a court of law after that confession.

I flip off my recording and give Blain another big hug. For once, I know exactly who I am and what I want. I'm the girl who doesn't give up, and I help others to the top.

"Are you sure you don't want to try it?" Woon says, pointing at the giant rollercoaster.

He wanted to take me somewhere romantic, and he did. Shijingshan Amusement Park is a major Disney rip-off, but the castle is pretty cool. I'm sure riding that rollercoaster would cross off the Do-Something-That-Makes-Me-Uncomfortable item on my list, but I'm counting my whole rescue effort instead. Rollercoasters are almost boring in comparison.

"Oppa," I say. I'm not entirely sure why he wants me to call him that, but I like the way it sounds as it rolls off my tongue. I pointing to giant flower-shaped cotton candy. “Why don’t we try some of that?”

“All right, fine.” He laughs. “Since it’s the last day.”

I really wish he wouldn’t remind me. Today’s almost gone and tomorrow he flies back to Korea, all of CSTAR’s filth exposed.

My phone recording has over a million views on YouTube. I think it’s safe to say Woon’s name is cleared. I’ll stay here and finish the school year. I’ve missed a few classes– thanks to him–but I think I can catch up.

He walks close to me that familiar smell of rice, honey, and spices wafting my way. Woon has been a bit of my home away from home. I don’t know what I’ll do without him.

“Hey,” Woon says, lifting my chin. “This isn’t the end.”

“I know,” I say, swallowing my emotions. “It’s just been so wonderful.”

It’s been a week since Woon was freed from CSTAR. We’ve spent every moment we have together, as have Blain and G.O. They even came to the park with us, but they're off doing their own thing. My only regret is that Woon and I haven't kissed again. We've never been totally alone with Blain and G.O. around.

I wrap one arm around Woon's waist and stare in his eyes. "Thanks for everything."

It feels so good to be in his arms, to be free to touch him like this. I wish it could last forever.

"That sounds an awful lot like a goodbye," he says. "I refuse to say goodbye to you."

A goodbye is inevitable. It's tomorrow. There's no avoiding it.

"Woon," I say with a sigh.

He puts a finger up. "Nope. Not going to do it."

I laugh. If only he knows how much I wish we could stay together.

He tugs my hand and starts to pull me away. "I have a surprise for you."

I bite my lip and raise my eyes to the beautiful clear sky. It's one of the few times it's been clear enough to breathe fresh air. It's like the heavens are blessing my last night with Woon.

He leans forward and whispers, "Wait here." Then he's gone. The amusement park crowd filters past, and I lose sight of his retreating frame.

I have no choice but to trust him. I stand still, waiting for him to return. Bright lights flash on, directing my attention to a stage set in the middle of an intersection.

I approach, noticing G.O. playing a guitar. He sends soothing bass vibes through the perfect night. Blain is at the bottom of the stage, her hair teal today, wearing her usual colorful leggings and combat boots. Turns out, G.O. liked her just the way she was.

Woon comes out and Blain gives me a nudge when she sees me blushing. He takes the stage and grabs the microphone. There's someone else I've seen before–I think his name is Yangbin–playing an electric guitar. It picks up, sending one tingling chord into the air.

Woon starts singing, and chills run up my arms, warming and cooling me at the same time. I know this song. I never thought I would like someone else singing my favorite Ed Sheeran song, but Woon hits each note perfectly. I cover my mouth and walk closer to the stage until I'm gripping the edge. Woon makes eye contact with me as he sings the words, *I'm in love now*. As if the title to the song—Kiss Me—wasn't romantic enough, each word he sings soaks through my ears and hits me in the heart.

Every bit of me trembles as I take in his meaning. He wants me with him, and I want to be there. Yangbin plays a guitar solo, and Woon pulls me onto the stage. Each high note is perfect, his voice better than a choir of angels. And he's all mine.

The song peters out as we stare into each other's eyes. The second the music dies, he pulls me close to his body and captures my lips in his mouth.

The world disappears. Even if my mom was watching, I still wouldn't stop kissing him. Not for anyone.

His fingers feel the muscles in my back as I push my lips to him harder, faster. Our breaths meld together, the wind swirling around us and holding us until we're one. His lips taste like sugar and lemon, sweet and sour, the perfect balance of flavors. My hands rub his shoulders, taking him all in. This man is mine. Doesn't matter how far away we are, he's giving himself to me, and I'm giving myself to him. We are meant to be.

He pulls away, and the crowd cheers below. "I'm never saying goodbye," he says, pulling a paper out of his back pocket. "Finish your schooling here, but then I want to take care of you for as long as I can."

It's a plane ticket to Korea. I know I'll use it, and I can't wait to be with him again.

"One last thing," he says, taking another paper out of his other pocket. "I didn't think I could leave until I gave you this." He unfolds it, and I recognize my handwriting.

It's my list. I have no idea how he got it. I haven't looked at it since I went to the street market that night.

1. ~~Visit the Great Wall of China~~
2. Do something that makes me uncomfortable
3. ~~Eat a crazy food from a street vendor~~
4. ~~Skip class~~

5. Fall in love

I stare at number five where Woon's handwriting is scrawled next to mine.

5. Fall in love – *I love you, Jenica. Do you love me?*

Tears fill my eyes, and this time, they spill over, dropping wet on the page. "Yes, Woon." I say. "I love you, always will."

He grabs the paper and pulls out a pen to scratch through number five. I still his hand, gripping it tight.

"Don't," I say. "Falling in love is more than a to-do list. It's something I want to keep doing with you, forever."

He takes me in his arms and spins me around, and I know no matter what we'll work through it. No more plans. No more calculations. Just love.

If you loved this book please review it!

Acknowledgements

Thank you dear reader, for taking the time to pick up this book. It's been a five-and-a half-year journey from the time I declared myself a writer to the time I finally had the courage to hit publish. Without you, the journey would be meaningless. I would love to hear your reviews as well.

A huge thank you to my husband who supported me even when he was overworked and tired. He was the first one to encourage me every time I wanted to give up, and for that I'll be eternally grateful. It's a good thing we're married forever. I have to mention my kids, too, since they constantly fuel my imagination with their own. As hard as it is to be a mom, I wouldn't trade it for anything.

Many, many thanks to Jenny Morris for reading this as a fanfic and telling me I had to publish it, and also for being the first beta reader. You're like a sister to me, and I couldn't imagine my life without you.

Clean Indie Reads has become one of my favorite Facebook groups and they helped me with the title. They are all incredible people.

Precy Larkins is the amazing editor for this work. I couldn't imagine having a better person to help make my book baby shiny. She's ten times the writer I am, and she's not afraid to give it to me straight. Thanks for being one of the best people on the planet.

Shout out to my author publishing group, Roxbury Books. I'm really excited to work with so many other talented writers to bring more Asian and K-Pop/K-Drama fiction to the world. Thank you Erica Laurie for starting it!

I couldn't write this without mentioning the real Jenica Lee whose name I stole to write this work. I'm glad she wanted me to write a fanfic for her so I could base the Jenica in this story off her. You could say she was my muse.

My Google Plus crew also needs a mention since they're the ones who started me writing fanfic when I thought I was too old to be doing such things. Especially Vee since she's been the greatest of friends. You all are the bomb!

Thank you to my best friend and critique partner Shelly Brown. She not only writes with me and encourages me every day, but she supports me in everything crazy including Kpop and Kdrama. Thanks Shelly for being the first one to watch Flower Boy Ramen shop after I told you it was good!

Shout out to my Beta Book Peeps who let me into their critique group when they didn't have to, and helped me become the writer I am today. Jenny Morris, Cassie Mae, Teresa Marie, Kelly Lynn, Suzi Retzlaff, Jessica Salyer, Lizzy Charles, Leigh Covington, and Hope Roberson. I love you all!!

And I can't end my acknowledgements without thanking my Father in Heaven. He gave me everything, and a little thanks is not enough to repay.

ABOUT THE AUTHOR

Jennie Bennett is a wife to a handsome and kind husband and a mother to four beautiful and crazy children. She found a passion in Korean pop culture in January of 2013 and she's never looked back since. She currently resides in Houston, Texas with her husband, kids, and a cute puppy named Charlie.

Twitter: @jabennettwrites

Facebook: Jennie Bennett

Instagram: @jenniefire

Come join my newsletter and get free books!

https://www.subscribepage.com/b3f6u5

Made in the USA
Monee, IL
23 August 2020